NEO ARCANA

STORIES

BRIAN ASMAN

A MUTATED MEDIA PRODUCTION

Neo Arcana: Stories
Copyright © 2022 Brian Asman

All Rights Reserved

ISBN: 978-1-7364677-5-6

The story included in this publication is a work of fiction. Names, characters, places and incidents are products of the author's imagination or are used fictitiously. Any resemblance to actual events or locales or persons living or dead is entirely coincidental.

Without limiting the rights under copyright reserved above, no part of this publication may be reproduced, stored in or introduced into a retrieval system, or transmitted, in any form, or by any means (electronic, mechanical, photocopying, recording, or otherwise), without the prior written permission of the copyright owner.

Cover Art by Kristina Osborn/Truborn Design

Interior Layout by Lori Michelle
www.TheAuthorsAlley.com

PRAISE FOR BRIAN ASMAN

"[In *I'm Not Even Supposed to Be Here Today*] the world just goes straight to hell, and takes you along with it. I haven't had this much fun watching terrible stuff happen in a long time."

—Stephen Graham Jones,
author of *My Heart is a Chainsaw*

"["A Festival of Fiends" is an] exceptional offering . . . sacrifice[s] neither storytelling nor style in realizing [its] thought-provoking concepts."

—*Publishers Weekly*

"Highly visual and cinematic worldbuilding"

—*Booklife by Publishers Weekly*

"Absolutely delivers . . . [in *Man, Fuck This House*] Asman took the standard haunted house tropes, poured some gasoline on them, and set them ablaze. Then he took the ashes, spread them around crazy town, and put it all back together to end his book. Holy wow."

—HorrorDNA.com

"[*Man, Fuck This House*] brilliantly subverts the standard haunted house cliches, ratcheting up the dread and bizarre circumstances toward a climax that makes King's "The House on Maple Street" seem normal . . . One of my favorite reads of the year."

—Duncan Ralston,
author of *Woom* and *The Ghostland Trilogy*

"Frenetic pacing, hilarious comedy, and inventive dialogue . . . [Asman] unleashes some suspense-building tricks worthy of King or Barker"
—Nick Kolakowski,
author of *Payback is Forever* and *Love & Bullets*

"A whirlwind of a ride . . . moments of mirth, moments of WTF."
—Janine Pipe,
author of *Twisted: Tainted Tales*

ALSO BY BRIAN ASMAN

I'm Not Even Supposed to Be Here Today
(Eraserhead Press)
Jailbroke
Nunchuck City
Man, Fuck This House

TABLE OF CONTENTS

Seven Years Bad Luck 1

Faces of Death 24

Stool Pigeon 39

The Siren Song of Sharp and Deadly Things 54

Moonboy..63

Preservation 83

Ghosts of Fredericksburg 103

For Thomas Ligotti, who taught me when one feels as if there's nowhere to go, nothing to do, and no one to know, there's no harm in keeping on anyway

SEVEN YEARS BAD LUCK

THEY FOUND HIM in the bathroom—razor blade in hand, slumped against the wall, shirtless in black boxer briefs, half his face slathered with shaving cream. A cruel red line etched across his neck, blood weeping down his lightly-furred chest, crimson rivulets running over the slight concavity between his nipples.

His pupils looked like dirty marbles in his skull.

Minutes before, his mother had stood outside the bathroom, heard the sound of the shower, seen the steam creeping under the door. Knocked twice, told the boy to hurry up, or he'd be late for school. He'd never actually been late for school, but his mother regarded her knocking as some sort of prophylactic against that very possibility.

Then she'd gone down and joined her husband in the kitchen, who was eating a banana and scrolling through his phone. Later they both agreed they'd heard the shower turn off, a detail likely misremembered because who would notice such a thing? Especially in a multi-story McMansion, with three and a half full baths and the boy's younger sister blasting a Toasters song from her room.

What they definitely noticed was his absence at the breakfast table. Well after his Cookie Crisp turned to mush in its bowl, their son had not come downstairs. Assuming the sort of assumptions one makes about teenage boys, but perhaps still possessed of primal instincts that breathily whispered the wrongness of the situation in their coddled ears, they walked up the lushly-carpeted stairs and knocked on the door to the bathroom the boy used exclusively.

No answer came from within.

Then a barrage of fiercer knocking, shouts asking if he was okay. Still, no reply came. With visions of their only son lying prone on the bathroom floor, knocked unconscious after falling out of the tub, his father turned the knob and the door swung open.

And then they *saw*.

First the mirror, steam-clouded but for a hand-swipe across the middle. Next the boy, bloodied and still against the opposite wall. For some unknown reason he'd shaved half his face before taking his own life, almost as though the act of shaving itself had convinced him of the Sisyphean pointlessness of human existence and he'd suddenly said *no more*.

At the far end of the hall, their only daughter, and now sole child, finally registered their screams over the blaring horns she always listened to as she brushed her hair. Rolling her eyes (teenagers, right?), she set her brush down on top of the dresser and went to see what was the matter.

Grant Gulden knew there was something wrong the first time Sasha brought him back to her place.

He'd suspected something might be off anyway since she was a real, live girl who seemed genuinely interested in him. They'd met on one of those dating apps, the kind that always felt like shopping. Does this one look appetizing? Swipe right for yes, left for no, maybe after reading a few sparse details about their interests. He found a lot of women didn't bother writing profiles, preferring to let their pictures do all the talking. Which put him in a jam, since he wanted to open with something more thoughtful than "Hey" or, even worse, "You're hot."

Grant didn't care for online dating, but then he hadn't been having much luck in the real world either. He'd chatted with a few girls online, went on a handful of dates. Nothing special, but striking out electronically didn't carry the same weight as striking out at a bar. The worst that could happen was some girl wouldn't message him back.

After he'd matched up with Sasha, they'd gone back and forth a little bit, talking about regular hiking trails, favorite animals, where they'd grown up, her visceral hatred of ska of any wave. He asked her out to a coffee shop, but she wanted to meet at a park instead. Which worked out nicely. Grant brought a blanket and a bottle of wine, and they enjoyed a cozy afternoon reclining on a great green slope overlooking downtown San Diego, watching dogs and their tennis ball-tossing owners merrily violate the leash laws.

He thought he'd made a mistake when he went to kiss her. She turned her head away for a moment. As he opened his mouth to apologize for being too forward, she'd turned back and kissed him square on the lips.

"I'm sorry," she said, pulling away. "It's just, it's been a while. Since I've dated anyone."

"I get it."

They went on a few more dates. The beach, hiking. A couple of times he suggested a wine bar, but Sasha demurred, saying she'd rather be outside.

Grant didn't much care. He was happy just to be with her.

A few dates in, still wet and salty from kayaking the cove, Sasha asked him back to her place.

She lived in a one-bedroom walk-up a few blocks from the beach. Grant followed her in, the cramped living room awash in floral scents. All the blinds were drawn, and Grant blinked for a moment until Sasha flipped on the overhead lights. The living room had a couch and a chair, no television. A few unframed posters lined the walls, the kind of prints found in the home of anyone with a casual interest in art history: Monet, Manet, Rembrandt. A large bookshelf dominated one wall, serving as both furniture and explanation for the lack of television.

"Do you want to shower first?" Grant said, hesitating on the linoleum just inside the door, horribly aware of both his presence in a woman's home for the first time and his wet board shorts under the towel wrapped around his waist.

"You can go first," Sasha said, blue eyes somehow brighter underneath her damp, blonde hair. "I kind of drip-dried on the way back. Salty though."

"Thanks," Grant said, hefting his backpack in one hand and hot-footing it across the carpet to the open door of the bathroom. Kayaking was the perfect date—physical, cooperative, and a great excuse to bring along a change of clothes.

"There's extra towels in the big drawer," Sasha called through the door.

"Thanks," Granted replied, opening the vanity and

SEVEN YEARS BAD LUCK

pulling out a neatly folded and deliciously fluffy purple towel from on top of the stack. As he stood up straighter, he noticed something odd about the bathroom.

There wasn't a mirror.

The medicine cabinet door had been removed from the cut-out that held all manner of cosmetics, lotions, and bottles, a pair of lonely and rust-bitten hinges marking the place where it had once been attached.

He looked around the room for another mirror. *Weird,* he thought. *Maybe she's a vampire. Ha.*

Then he showered and waited on the couch while she showered and they got to know each other better.

Days turned into weeks. Sasha and Grant grew closer, going for walks on the beach, kayaking, making love at her place. It was a good routine. Grant's arms and stomach grew taut, his skin gained a healthy glow. He even started reading again, after he'd complained one night about not being able to watch the Padres game and Sasha pushed a novel called *Ghostland* into his hands.

They were getting to the point where somebody was going to have to say, "Hey, are we boyfriend and girlfriend or what?"

Two things stopped Grant from asking that question.

The first was that she never wanted to go to his place. Hers *was* closer to the beach. But in a month she'd never come over. He'd asked her a few times and she'd always made up some reason why they needed to spend the night at hers. She had to be at work early, even though she'd never explained exactly what she did for a living.

The second was that she'd only met his friends in passing. Every time his friends planned a happy hour or a night out, even bowling, Sasha always had something to do the next day.

"You can go," she'd tell him. "Have fun with your friends, you can come over after."

But the idea of abandoning the smattering of freckles across the bridge of her nose for his dumbass friends always made him text them *sorry, another time*.

One night, driving back from a hike up El Capitan, Sasha riding scrunched down in the passenger seat with her knees up against the side window like she always did, Grant decided to push things.

"Babe, let's go to my place tonight."

Sasha tensed up next to him. "I've got those Thai leftovers we should eat. They might not last another day."

Thai food they'd ordered in. Grant wondered sometimes if she was agoraphobic, except that didn't square with the hiking and kayaking.

"Come on," Grant said, putting on his best smile. "It'll be fun. You've never even seen my place."

Sasha wrapped her arms around his and nuzzled her face into his shoulder. "You come on. Think of the pineapple-fried rice."

"What if I make dinner?"

She gave his shoulder a bite through his flannel shirt. "What if you *are* dinner?"

"Is there something wrong with my place? We never hang out there. Let's just make dinner, I'll grill some Mahi, and then I'll give you a ride home if you don't want to stay."

Sasha sighed. "I just like my place, that's all. You're right though, it's not fair we always go to mine. I guess we can go to yours tonight. It'll be fine. Fun."

Grant looked over. Sasha was staring at the floor mat, massaging her temples. Her lips moving, silently whispering to herself.

An affirmation. A lie.

As soon as they walked in the door to his apartment, Sasha seemed skittish, like he'd talked her into breaking into a derelict house or something. Her shoulders quaked beneath her thin woolen sweater.

"It's okay, babe, I really live here. Promise."

"Yeah, it's, uh, nice," Sasha said, her eyes scanning the room without landing on anything.

Grant set his bag down by the door. "You can grab a seat on the couch while I get dinner started. You want anything to drink?" He glanced up when she didn't respond. "Sasha?"

She was staring at the couch. A typical brown felt three-seater, neither particularly nice nor particularly dirty. He wondered if she was thinking about how many other girls might have sat on it.

There weren't that many.

"Why don't I just help you cook dinner?" Sasha said.

"Uh, sure." Grant walked into the kitchen, or rather over to it, since the kitchen and living room were separated by a chest-high breakfast bar covered in mail and a wire basket full of bananas.

"Banana? You know, for the potassium?"

Sasha shook her head. "I'll wait for the Mahi. How about some wine in the meantime?"

Grant poured them each a glass of pinot noir. Sasha seemed to relax a little.

Maybe she just likes being at home, Grant thought.

They spent the next half hour cooking dinner and chatting. Sasha seemed more like herself. After he'd filled their plates with pan-fried fish, veggie stir fry and rice, Grant asked if she wanted to pick out a movie to watch while they ate.

Sasha blanched, her plate jiggling in her hands. "No, why don't we just—I know! Let's sit here at the breakfast bar. Then we can talk. And drink?"

Grant appraised her for a moment, then nodded. "Yeah, okay, let me move this mail out of the way."

He scooped up a handful of letters and coupons and looked around the apartment before depositing them on the kitchen counter.

"I'll go through that later."

"Right."

Maybe Grant wasn't the greatest cook, but the meal was decent and the company even better. They talked about everything and nothing, trifles from childhood, like the Little League trophy Grant won after hitting a double in the bottom of the ninth with two men on. The Louisville Slugger he'd swung that day hung above his couch, an artifact that had survived over twenty years of lesser achievements to retain its place of pride in the living room. Grant told her about Christmases and birthdays, songs he'd liked in seventh grade, dumb things he'd gotten into with his buddies from college. His wine-addled mind was dimly aware of how little she was sharing herself, but Sasha kept prompting him, seemingly wanting to know every last minute detail about his life.

After dinner they opened another bottle and Sasha tried to insist on cleaning their plates, but he wouldn't have it.

Not long after that, they went to bed.

Grant woke up in the middle of the night, covers tangled around his waist, Sasha on her stomach next to him. His left arm was dead asleep. Careful not to wake her, he slowly pulled his arm out from under her neck and sat up.

A few shakes later, pins and needles swarmed his arm. He'd forgotten the downsides of sleeping with someone else. The balled-up underwear on the floor next to the bed reminded him of the upsides.

A faint, murmuring noise drew his attention. Sasha was muttering something in her sleep. Some sort of sing-songy refrain. He leaned closer, his ear hovering over her lips.

"If you see you . . . then you'll see me . . . tra la la, tra la di . . ."

Grant shook his head. *Weird*. Just another one of Sasha's quirks. She seemed to have a never-ending supply of them, but then again there she was, lying on her stomach in one of his old t-shirts, moonlight from between the blinds highlighting her butt cheeks.

He pulled on his boxers and went to the bathroom, leaving the light off so he'd hopefully fall back asleep. He took a piss, trying his best to aim in the dark. It wouldn't do for Sasha to wake up and find urine all over everything.

BRIAN ASMAN

Reasonably certain he'd kept it in the bowl, he flushed the toilet and turned on the faucet. Bending over the sink, he filled his hands with water and took a drink. As he stood up, he caught a glimpse of himself in the darkened mirror.

Something moved behind him.

Grant yelped, jumping and reaching for the light. A flick of the switch ignited the overheads. Nothing behind him. He paused for a moment, straining to hear anything over the sound of his own breathing.

Nothing in the bathroom but the soft gurgle of the toilet.

Grant laughed to himself. Nerves, spawned from a few hours of drunk-sleep and the novelty of actually having a woman sleeping in his bed again. One he liked, even.

He glanced back at the mirror. Nothing but the familiar beige wall behind him, the towel bar strung with a mauve towel he wished he'd remembered to wash. And him, looking bleary-eyed and disheveled.

Nerves, he thought.

Tap.

He jerked away from the sink, looked around the room. The pipes, maybe? These were older apartments, built in the '80s, and—

Tap.

Almost sounded like the noise was coming from the mirror. Grant leaned over the sink, listening. He grabbed some bunched-up toilet paper and laid a hand on the cabinet, skin crawling at the thought of a roach or water bug crawling all over his toiletries.

Tap.

The noise drew his attention back to the mirror. He looked past his disheveled appearance, a slight

SEVEN YEARS BAD LUCK

motion pulling his gaze down to the bottom of the mirror.

Where a single elongated fingernail, slathered in glitter and purple and yellow nail polish, tapped the mirror again.

From the inside.

Grant stumbled backward, the towel bar jabbing into his spine, gaping at that horrible nail tapping on the wrong side of the glass. Other nails joined it, clicking their way into view from the bottom of the mirror, skittering up the surface and then a hand, pale and veiny and perversely stretched out like in a funhouse mirror.

The nails kept tapping on the inside of the mirror until they reached the top and paused. Right on the reflection of his hairline. Veins pulsed in the wrist, thumping in time to the same rhythm the nails tapped out.

He looked up, didn't see anything above him.

Suddenly the hand descended, dragging its nails along the face of the mirror, a shrill squeak emanating from the glass like a blackboard except far, far louder.

Grant covered his ears and screamed.

Sasha rushed into the bathroom, something black and orange in her hand. She lunged forward, plunging the object into the center of the mirror.

Shattering it.

The horrible sound from the mirror stopped. Shards cascaded down the wall and into the sink. Grant realized he was still screaming and clapped a hand over his mouth until he got himself under control.

"Hand me the wastebasket," Sasha shouted over her shoulder.

Grant gaped at her.

"The trash can, now!" she repeated.

Moving mechanically, his limbs stiff and heavy, Grant picked up the small black trash can from between the tub and the toilet and handed it to her.

Sasha cradled the wastebasket under one arm, the side of her breast squishing into the plastic edge, picking shards out of the sink and tossing them in. "I knew it, I knew it, I knew it," she muttered.

Grant watched her work, hands hanging at his sides. His mind was a buzzing hornet's nest of questions, different thoughts fighting each other as they tried to make their way to his lips. Instead, he said nothing.

"Ow, shit!" Sasha brought a finger up to her mouth and sucked on it.

"Cut yourself on the glass?" Grant said, taking a step closer to the sink.

She had not. The remaining shards in the porcelain sink roiled with dozens of tiny hands, all bearing the same painted fingernails. All of them reaching out of the broken glass, slashing the air.

"What the hell?" Grant said.

"Hand me that towel."

Grant yanked the towel so hard he ripped the rack from the wall, sending flecks of dust and drywall spiraling towards the ceiling. He passed her the towel, his racing mind somehow still catching the slight musty smell.

He really should have washed it before he had her over.

Sasha wrapped the towel around her hand and reached back into the sink, scooping up the shards and throwing them in the wastebasket. "What other mirrors do you have in the house?"

SEVEN YEARS BAD LUCK

"Mirrors?" he replied dumbly.

"Yes, fucking mirrors, Grant. How many mirrors do you have?"

"Uh—" Grant ticked them off on his fingers. "I think there's one on my dresser. In the bedroom."

"Go get it. No others?"

He shook his head. "I don't think so."

"Okay. Bring it here and smash it in the sink. And whatever you do, don't look in it."

Grant raced back through the apartment and into his bedroom, nearly tripping over a pile of clothing on the floor. He righted himself and grabbed the hand mirror off his dresser by its plastic handle, angling it downwards, careful not to look in it.

As he walked into the bathroom, something stung the bare flesh of his thigh. A single finger protruded from the underside of the hand mirror, a fat droplet of his blood sliding down the nail.

Before he could scream Sasha grabbed the mirror out of his hands and smashed it in the sink. With the towel, she picked those pieces up and tossed them in the wastebasket.

"You don't have a safe or anything, do you?" she asked.

Grant shook his head. "No. No safe."

"Okay, um, we'll put this in the dishwasher."

"Dishwasher?"

"It locks, doesn't it? Look, once the mirror's smashed she can't come all the way *out*. More an annoyance than anything else."

Grant looked down at the red slash on his thigh. He balled up some toilet paper and pressed it against the wound.

"You still don't want these shards around," Sasha

continued. "Damn it, I really thought I was safe. I shouldn't have come here. It's been years, since—"

Everything clicked for Grant. He'd listened to a podcast about this thing that happened in Colorado, years before. The details fit.

A group of teenagers, dead. Forensics that didn't even come close to adding up.

And a handful of survivors, all irrationally afraid of mirrors. *Eisotrophobia,* he remembered the podcast host calling it.

"You were there. Holy shit."

Just my luck, he thought. *I finally meet someone and she's goddamn cursed.*

Sasha finished tossing the mirror fragments in the trashcan, wrapping the towel tightly around it. "Here."

"Okay, dishwasher it is," he said, taking the can.

She nodded. "Are you sure you don't have any other mirrors in the house?"

Grant shook his head. "I mean, I'm a guy."

"Asshole."

Grant went into the kitchen and opened the dishwasher. The bottom drawer was full of pots with dried macaroni stuck to the bottom, plates with tacky multi-colored stains. He set the trash can down and emptied the bottom drawer. Tried to ignore the scrabbling noises coming from underneath the towel. Once he'd made enough room, he put the trashcan in the dishwasher and locked the door.

He poked his head into the bathroom. Sasha was leaning over the toilet, panting heavily, blonde hair hanging ragged on either side of her face.

"Here," he said, pulling her hair back.

"I'm fine," she said, but didn't pull away. She

retched again. Only a thin sliver of drool came out. She wiped it away with the back of her hand.

"What do we do now? Go out for breakfast?" Grant asked with a weak smile.

"Not funny."

Something clunked under the sink.

Sasha's head whipped up. "What was that?"

Grant eyed the cabinet. "Water in the pipes?"

The sound came again.

"That's not water," Sasha said, pushing off the toilet rim and clambering to her knees. "I thought you said you didn't have any more mirrors."

"I don't. Except—oh, shit."

"What?"

"There's a little hand mirror in my Dopp kit."

The thumping sounds underneath the sink increased in tempo.

"Get your bat."

Grant ran to the living room and snatched his old Slugger from its mount on the wall, then back to the bathroom. Sasha waited next to the vanity, a hand poised on the knob of the cabinet.

"Hopefully she's still in your Dopp kit. When I open the door, smash that fucking thing. You got it?"

Grant nodded, glad Sasha still had her wits about her. Otherwise, he'd probably have just stood there while those multi-colored fingernails sliced him to bits.

"Now!" Sasha flung the cabinet open. Something was moving inside the Dopp kit, probing the faux leather. Seeking a way out.

With the tip of the bat, Grant swept the bag from beneath the sink. It flopped onto the floor, the thing within still moving. A fingernail pierced the side and sliced the bag open. The rip widened, revealing fingers moving amongst the travel-size bottles of toothpaste and shaving cream.

He brought the bat down once, twice, three times, smashing the shit out of his bag. The fingers disappeared.

But somewhere within, tiny hands were emerging from the shards.

"Throw it in the dishwasher too, I guess?"

"Yeah. Just be careful."

Grant set the bat on the sink and stooped to pick up the bag. The tear looked like an angry mouth, ready to consume any flesh that strayed too near. He gingerly held the bag by a corner. Little hands caromed like roaches within.

As he rounded the corner into the living room, he saw himself reflected in the empty television screen. And then something else stepped into the frame.

The thing in the TV looked like a drunken child's drawing of a human being. The head was queerly shaped, stretched and smooshed, chin and forehead flowing in different directions. Its arms were long and narrow, fingers pointed like blades, while its midsection was perversely rotund.

For the second time that night, Grant screamed.

Sasha lunged into the living room, brandishing his bat. "Where? Where is she?"

Grant pointed a trembling finger at the monstrous figure that stood next to his own reflection. "There."

Sasha glanced at the TV. "Oh. There she is. Huh." She made no move to swing the bat.

Grant looked at her, bewildered. "Aren't you going to—"

Sasha shrugged. "She only comes out of mirrors.

SEVEN YEARS BAD LUCK

I don't like looking at her, though. Why I don't have a TV."

"Huh." The twisted thing in the television stared back at him, impotent and malevolent at the same time. "How is this even possible, I mean what—"

"Your Dopp kit."

He looked down at the bag. "Oh yeah." He locked the bag in the dishwasher with his wastebasket.

Sasha turned the TV around on its stand so it faced the wall and sat down on the couch. "I didn't smash it," she said. "I figure you can still sell it."

"Sell it?"

Sasha nodded. "Well, yeah. Unless you like looking at her every time you walk in the living room."

"Every time—"

"And you'll have to comb your hair by feel. You're a guy, I don't know, maybe you can get a buzz cut or something. Yeah," she continued, brightening, "you'd probably look pretty sexy with short hair."

Grant ran a hand through his hair, unkempt from hours of sleep. "Wait, you mean—"

Sasha's face fell. "Yeah. I fucked up. I shouldn't have gotten you into this. I thought I was free," Sasha said, more to herself than Grant. "I wasn't even involved, it was my stupid brother and his friends. Thought it would be funny, giving this girl bunk X and locking her in the House of Mirrors for the night at our high school carnival. Except it wasn't bunk, and they gave her too much. Way too much."

"I read once," Grant said, his voice sounding foreign in his own ears, "back in Victorian times when someone died they covered all the mirrors in the house."

"A bunch of cultures do. Turns out there's a reason for it."

Grant opened his mouth, to say something, anything, but Sasha cut him off. "I just thought, I don't know, it's been years since everything happened. And I've been so careful. You've seen my place. I don't go anywhere there might be mirrors, like bars. I started carrying around that Lifehammer in my purse, just in case. I even keep my blinds drawn, so I don't ever see her reflected in the window. I've never actually *seen* her, until tonight. But now I know she's after me. And she's seen you."

Grant sighed and sat down next to her on the couch. "I guess I'm fucked, then."

She patted his knee. "It's not so bad. At least you won't have to learn how to put on makeup by feel. I probably looked like the fucking Joker for the first few months." She exhaled heavily. "I am sorry, though. I wouldn't wish something like this on anyone. Especially someone I care about. I'm not going to lie, it's hard, living like this. But, what am I supposed to do, never date anyone again? Live life like a nun or something?"

Grant looked at her, feeling tears well up. Whatever he thought about his current situation, and he hadn't even begun to consider what the implications for the rest of his life might be, seemed so much less important than the look in Sasha's eyes.

He forced a smile, hoping it would appear genuine enough. "You were worth it."

Sasha leaned in and kissed him. "God, I hope so. You know, I don't get it though. Why she came tonight."

Something clicked in Grant's head. "You were singing. This little rhyme, in your sleep. Something about seeing you, seeing me?"

SEVEN YEARS BAD LUCK

"Wait, in my sleep? God damn—"

Something crashed on the other side of the wall.

Someone screamed. And kept screaming, the noise mostly muffled by the wall, sounding strange and far away.

They jumped off the couch. Sasha and Grant stood side-by-side, baseball bat in Sasha's hands, regarding the living room wall.

"My neighbor," Grant said lamely. The screaming cut out with a jarring finality.

"We have to leave."

"And go where?"

"Anywhere. The mountains. Out to the desert. Somewhere without mirrors."

Grant looked around his apartment. Wondered if he'd ever see it again. "Let me just grab—"

A hand burst through the wall and they both screamed.

Another smashed through, candy-striped fingernails swiping viciously at the air. Hands grabbed the edges of the holes they'd made and pulled. Making them bigger.

"Sasha—"

The wall ripped open. They jumped over the couch, staying away from those probing fingers.

Something inside of the wall was singing. Grant froze for a moment, one foot perched on the arm of the couch. Listening.

If I see you, you'll see me, tra la la, tra la di.

"Grant," Sasha yelled and ran for the door.

Grant snapped out of his reverie and followed, snatching his keys and wallet off the table. They ran outside to his car. The sky was turning pink, the first rays of dawn emerging to the east.

Behind them, his neighbor's door burst open.

They reached the car in seconds. Sasha cocked back the bat and shattered the mirror on the passenger's side. The car alarm went off, the horn honking and lights flashing. She ran around the front of the car and took out the driver's side mirror.

"Get the rearview mirror, Grant!"

Grant hit the unlock button on the fob and the alarm stopped. He threw open the door and leaned in. A hand emerged from the rearview mirror. He grabbed the sides of the mirror, and with a strength born of pure hysteria ripped it from the windshield, spinning around and spiking it on the ground like a football.

Sasha was already sliding into the passenger seat. "Let's go, hurry."

Grant jumped into the car, jabbed his key at the ignition for an interminable moment until the key finally slid home, and started the engine.

"Come on," Sasha yelled, slapping the dash.

Grant pulled out as fast as he could, nearly clipping the bumper of the car parked in front of him, then floored it. At the end of the block, he had to slow down to turn. Sasha whipped her head around, looking out the back window.

"Is she back there?"

Sasha shook her head. "No. Nothing."

Grant exhaled a breath he hadn't realized he was holding. "Good."

Silently, they drove into the coming dawn.

SEVEN YEARS BAD LUCK

They dressed in mismatched, mildewed clothes from a gym bag Grant found in the backseat. When they stopped for gas and food, he parked at the pump furthest away from the other cars, to avoid the danger of their mirrors. Sasha ran in to get food and drinks. He hadn't wanted her to expose herself to the fisheye mirrors they probably had in the ceiling to deter pickpockets, but she wouldn't have it.

"I've been doing this for years," Sasha said. "I just stare at the floor, use my peripherals to make sure I'm not near any mirrors. We're away from her now, she won't find us unless one of us looks directly into one. Or we sing that fucking song in our sleep. I don't even remember where I first heard the thing, supposedly it was some nonsense her E-ed out self babbled into the mirror as she died." She muttered something that sounded like "stupid" before turning her back and walking into the store.

Standing there at the pump, Grant felt horribly exposed. He shivered every time a car passed out on the road, the early morning sun glinting off their sideview mirrors. He kept thinking how glad he was that his car didn't have chrome bumpers. It kept him from thinking about other things. Like how exactly life was going to work from here on out.

Sasha returned with bags stuffed with water, protein bars, and chips. "I bought all their bananas," she said, tearing one off the bushel and handing it to Grant.

Grant could only think about eating in the most academic of terms. He knew he'd have to eat, eventually, but he couldn't picture himself doing it.

"Thanks," he said, setting the banana on the dash. "I'll eat it later."

They drove through the mountains and down into the desert, neither entirely sure where they were going. Sometimes they talked, never of the thing that pursued them or their future, but trivialities of the past. Teachers they'd had, jobs they'd hated, television shows they'd seen as children. This time Sasha did most of the talking, Grant savoring every detail.

A few miles over the Arizona border, a siren blared. Grant craned his neck, caught the red and blue lights behind them.

"Damn it," he said. "I'm barely over the speed limit."

"Maybe they're looking for us."

"What? Why?"

"Your neighbor. All that screaming, somebody was bound to call the police."

Grant swallowed hard. He pulled to the shoulder, rolling down his window before killing the engine. He wanted to bang his head against the steering wheel until he lost consciousness and hopefully woke up in a world that actually made sense.

He pawed through the glove box for his papers. "I don't have my new insurance card."

They waited for the cop to come, hoping they'd simply fallen into a speed trap, that they weren't the subject of an APB. Without a rearview mirror, it was difficult to watch the cop's progress as he went through all his cop rituals.

Finally, the cop got out of his car. Heavy footsteps approached. Grant nervously fingered the papers in his lap.

"License, registration, and insurance, please."

Grant handed it through the window without

Seven Years Bad Luck

looking. "I don't have my insurance card. Can I just look it up on my phone?"

The cop said nothing for a moment, then "Do you know why I stopped you?"

Grant looked up at the cop, saw himself reflected in a pair of mirrored sunglasses.

He opened his mouth to reply—

But the fingernails lunging from the cop's shades silenced him.

FACES OF DEATH

THE NIGHT BEFORE her family took away the face she'd known for every last one of her twelve years, Maria lay in bed, listening to Diego mutter soft susurrations to dead girls through the thin wall separating her tiny room from his own. Sometimes he'd pause, the slight skritch-skritch of a mechanical pencil filling the silence, and Maria wondered what they said, who they'd been.

And how odd it must be, to be lost and dead and telling their secrets to a stranger.

She'd seen the notebooks Diego and the others used—black-and-white speckled, the same kind she worked out algebra problems in—but never peeked inside. The rest of the family guarded them jealously, locking them in a fireproof safe in Uncle Chris and Aunt Elaine's room alongside the deed to the house and her and Diego's birth certificates. When she was younger, she'd been curious, asked her aunt—and sometimes even her mother or father—how it all worked, what secrets the dead told. Why it fell to her family to listen to them in the first place, because the families on TV, the Pritchetts or the Johnsons or the Goldbergs, none of them talked to dead people.

Nor did their faces look anything like the Luna clan's.

FACES OF DEATH

She must've drifted off because Diego woke her before dawn. Moonlight reflected off his skeleton-white cheeks, his head hanging upside down from the top bunk where he used to sleep, lank black hair dangling off his skull like seaweed.

His warm, sleep-stale breath—even more like death than his face, Diego constantly frustrated Mother with his stubborn refusal to brush or floss before bed—buffeted her, rudely dragging her into the waking world with an already-twisting stomach.

"Today's the day," Diego sing-songed, grinning. "Are you excited?"

The only appropriate answer in their household was *of course,* so that's what Maria said.

Even if her tone didn't match the words.

"It's okay," Diego said. "It hurts. And afterwards, you can't play outside for like two weeks. And you have to rub this smelly lotion all over your cheeks."

"I'll be fine." The thought of what they'd do over the next couple of hours to make her face up like Diego's made her shiver, and she hoped it was too dark in her bunk for her brother to see the tiny convulsion.

Diego smirked. "Tough girl, huh? Bet you a dollar you'll cry."

Maria shrugged her blanket off, Mr. Fuzzle-Muzzle falling softly to the floor. "I'm not going to cry."

"Will too."

"I'm not a baby like you."

"That's funny, I didn't feel a thing."

"Liar." The night they'd taken her brother's old face, she'd stolen downstairs, padding across the floorboards in her pink footie pajamas. Drawn by voices, the stink of cigars smoked inside—unusual—and a strange, rhythmic buzzing, like a wasp hovering around a microphone. She'd known what was happening, of course, the Lunas didn't believe in wall-papering their children's world with soft, bright lies, a pastel paint smear over the ugliness beneath. Santa Claus never existed in their household, nor the Tooth Fairy, nor the Easter Bunny. And death was never euphemized with limp phrases like "passed away" or "gone to a better place."

After all, it was the family business.

A board by the couch creaked, and for a moment she feared she'd given herself away, Aunt Elaine would come bursting through the garage door and sweep her up in her lithe and powerful arms, inked from shoulder to fingertip with colorful depictions of Japanese demons.

But no one came. She followed the buzzing to the garage door, the splash of light underneath. Sniffed cigar smoke through the cracks. Heard music—Led Zeppelin—leaking through the door, the chatter of voices. Laughter.

Underneath it all, the constant, arrhymthic sobbing of a ten-year-old boy painfully realizing, pinprick by pinprick, that free will was a lie and everything that mattered in his universe was predestined, etched in stone and blood twenty thousand years or more before his conception.

Diego sneered at her now, sticking out his tongue. "I never cried. You weren't there for my masking." He leaned in, breath hot and heavy on her cheeks.

"But I'll be there for yours."

Maria hit him with her pillow until he, laughing and pretending to fend her off, lost his balance and hit the floor with a thud.

FACES OF DEATH

She brushed her teeth slowly. Unlike her brother, she'd always taken good care of her teeth, even ones she knew she'd soon lose. Obsessive, perhaps, but they did so much for her, and Maria was a girl overwhelmed at times by gratitude for the small and unacknowledged things around her, the things no one noticed until they stopped working. Her lungs, her heart, the tingly nerves in her fingertips that granted pleasure when she stroked one of Aunt Elaine's silk scarves, or pain when she grasped a stove-hot pan without thinking. And her appreciation was not strictly confined to her own body, her own senses—when she was seven, she learned without gravity they'd all float off into space, her and Diego and mother and father and Aunt Elaine and Uncle Chris, arms uselessly waving, faces growing blue, drifting farther apart, lost in the mind-numbingly expansive emptiness around them.

That whole next year, she said a prayer to gravity every night.

Maria spat in the sink, put her toothbrush away. Spent a long moment staring at herself in the mirror, letting her fingertips trace her jawline, run down her nose like a bead of sweat, poke the soft spaces beneath her eyes. She tapped on her brow, the low *dhk-dhk-dhk* resonating to her cheekbone.

Tomorrow, it would all be gone.

"Maria?" Aunt Elaine called from outside the door, rapping on the frame with her knuckles. "Are you ready?"

There was no other answer but yes.

They were all jammed into Uncle Chris' Tundra, bumping down a dirt road, she and Diego smooshed up against each other in the back, her mom in Father's lap, Aunt Elaine with her bare feet up on the dash in the passenger seat like some itinerant queen. They'd passed a lonely, rusted sign three or four miles back, unreadable from her anti-vantage point in the middle seat, Diego's big round head blocking the view. She was very, very tired of being the youngest, but there was nothing she could do about that.

Except murder her brother, but then he'd just come back to bug her even worse.

"I never thought I was a purple gal, but I think it suits me," Aunt Elaine said, wiggling her toes. "Do you like it?" She poked Uncle Chris' hand, but he brushed her off.

"Babe, I'm driving."

Aunt Elaine blew a raspberry, pretended to pout, but she couldn't even fool the twelve-year-old girl in the backseat, let alone her husband. As long as Maria could remember, her aunt and uncle's love was saccharine-sweat, so cloyingly particulate you couldn't sit in a room—or an extended cab Japanese truck, for that matter—without leaving feeling a little dirty.

Contrasted to her parents, whose own love was never questioned, and yet a secret thing, hardly on display. Their current physical proximity was a matter of convenience, nothing more. Both of the elder Lunas were taciturn, not exactly severe, just serious. Her father, a wiry bundle of scars who let his black hair grow long to shroud his face, spoke little, preferring to express himself with a gentle hand laid on her shoulder, a wry smile, an unexpected and personal gift—when she was nine, one morning at breakfast he pressed a wooden hummingbird into her hands he carved himself, and went out to feed the chickens when she tried to thank him.

Other than Aunt Elaine's nail polish monologue, no one else talked much—the ritual was later, but the Stone Run was preamble, and varying degrees of sacred to everyone in the car. Silence filled the cab because out here the radio antenna could only pull down static from the sky.

"Heard from Benitez," her father said, apropos of nothing. "Granderson's coming out of the coma. Supposably."

"Hrrm," Uncle Chris said. Paused so long someone unfamiliar with his peculiar cadences might've thought the subject settled, then said, "Goddamn cartel shit."

Maria's mother made a face but wasn't about to say anything in Uncle Chris' truck. Profanity was the one thing she tried to shield her children from—silly when they gave up their faces for life, and then their minds and bodies time and time again, until the world used them all up.

Uncle Chris turned down another unmarked road, and there they were before Maria even had time to think.

El cementerio.

Maybe it had a name, once, but no longer. A limestone wall circled the lonely half-acre, a rusted gate yawned open, becoming them inside. Overhead, the sun beat down from a cloudless sky, and the temperature on the dash display read in the mid-90s.

Uncle Chris pulled up just outside the gate and shut off the engine. "Here we are," he said redundantly.

There they were.

Maria's parents got out first, spilling out the right side, while Diego took his time, posturing and stinking of boy sweat. Finally Maria too. Uncle Chris and Aunt Elaine were already standing by the back of the truck, lowering the gate. Aunt Elaine pulled a cracked-leather handbag from the bed and slung it over her shoulder.

"Ready?"

Maria's stomach dropped. She wasn't, not for any of this. But her whole damn family, except for Uncle Ned, was standing there under the hot baking sun, cracked red clay beneath their feet, looking at her with awkward smiles, their bone-white faces and ink-whorled cheeks glistening in the early afternoon light. A drop of sweat ran down her father's brow. He wiped it away with a dirty bandana, never taking his eyes off her.

She nodded.

Aunt Elaine took her by the hand and led her away.

Into the cemetery.

Aunt Elaine's hand was warm in hers, and Maria was grateful for it. She pressed her wrist against her aunt's, felt the tiny drumbeat of a pulse. Her own beat faster.

They wended their way down a dusty path, overgrown with weeds and lined with gravestones. Tiny stones scattered beneath Maria's trainers. The air hung thick and hot around them.

"Never been in a graveyard before, have you?"

FACES OF DEATH

Maria shook her head.

"This is the easy part," Aunt Elaine said, nodding at the weathered, nearly-illegible hunks of stone littered around the dirt. "Lots to choose from. The trick is to pick just the right one."

"How's that?"

Aunt Elaine stopped, leaned down until her white nose was nearly tip-to-tip with Maria's. "You want to know what I did?"

Maria nodded.

"I thought about who each person was," she indicated the cemetery with a sweep of her tattooed arm, "and who I might want to be."

Maria squinted at the nearest grave marker—*Soleil Estevez, 1834-1869. Wife and Mother.* Even at twelve she knew those were both identities and duties, and wouldn't want her own life summed up by what she owed to others.

So, not that one.

"Take your time," Aunt Elaine said softly.

Maria did. She wandered the haphazard rows, inspecting what stones she could. Some had their legend worn away by the ravages of time, while others had toppled, and were too heavy for a girl of twelve to put right.

A few markers she dismissed easily—anyone who died younger than her wasn't someone she wanted to be. Others she lingered over, sounding out their names, trying the syllables on for size. "Bartholomew Crumbley," she said, picturing herself at the bathroom mirror, saying it over and over. Writing it at the top of a math test. Hearing it spoken over the intercom at a school to which she'd never return, or called out at an assembly for good grades.

Maria didn't know how long they wandered the graveyard. Aunt Elaine walked beside her without complaint, the cracked leather bag swinging in her hand. The sun blazed on, leaching every drop of moisture from Maria's throat. Aunt Elaine pressed a water bottle into her hand, and she drank deep.

"There's no rush," Aunt Elaine said. "This is important. It's a big choice."

And there it was, wasn't it? The moment the veil shifted, ever so slightly, giving Maria a glimpse of what lay beneath. The life of a child was one of prescription, every supposed decision trivial. Orange juice or RC Cola? Hamburgers or hot dogs? The yellow dress or the blue one?

Had Maria ever even made a real choice before? Decided anything of consequence?

She'd not chosen to be born, into this peculiar family or at all. Wasn't any choice that followed after simply the illusion of such? Did it matter which stone she chose, when her face would be taken from her either way?

"You know why we do this, don't you?" Aunt Elaine sat down by a tombstone, patted the ground next to her.

Maria sat as well, snuggling into the crook of her aunt's arm.

Aunt Elaine picked at the ground, snatching up a strand of crabgrass. Inspected it briefly, making a face as though it displeased her, then flung it away.

"You saw what I just did?"

Maria nodded.

"That blade of grass was nothing to me. I ripped it out of the ground for no reason at all and tossed it away. I'll go home tonight and lie in my bed and fall asleep without a thought. The only time I'll think of it again is if I'm reminiscing about the day I spent with my favorite niece."

Maria looked down at her shoes, blushing.

"Of course, you're my *only* niece, so it's not like you've much competition. But even if you did," and now Elaine slipped her fingers into Maria's armpits, and tickled with all the viciousness an adult can levy upon a child, "you'd *still* be my favorite!"

They collapsed on the red clay, giggling and laughing, tears streaming from their eyes—though Maria's laughter sounded hollow, and she realized she was making herself do it, and the tears were for another reason entirely.

When the mirth—real or not—passed, as all mirth does, Elaine looked deeply into Maria's eyes and said, "For some people, a person's just like that blade of grass. They rip them from the earth, away from their families. Toss them away without a thought, and sleep like a babe when the screaming's done. And that blade of grass—" and now she pointed, away across the hard-packed earth, directly at the blade she'd flung away, lying still against a weathered grave because the wind was so slight, so heat-weakened, it couldn't move it, "—lingers, lost, blowing where it will. Can you imagine being lost like that? Lost in the dark, with no one around, and no eyes to see and no voice to cry out?"

Maria shook her head. She couldn't imagine that, didn't want to.

Aunt Elaine ran a hand down her tattooed face. "All of us, me and your mother and father and Uncle Chris, even Diego, we're all beacons in the dark. We do this so they can *see* us. Do you understand?"

Maria looked up at her aunt, tracing the dark whorls around her eyes, her chin. The markings that made her look like a skeleton. Dead. Although her aunt always said, it was less the design, than what they were made of.

"Are you ready to pick one?" Aunt Elaine said, standing up and brushing graveyard dirt off her jeans.

Maria turned in a long, slow circle, surveying the graveyard. Must've been a thousand graves, more, each of them a life lost long before her father's father's father was born. Pioneers and peasants, vaqueros and ranchers. Many of them born somewhere else, traveling across a continent, only to settle here in this dusty red soil.

"If it makes it any easier," Aunt Elaine said, "you can't pick the wrong one. We choose so we feel like we're a part of the process, but the dust? The dust is what we need. All that matters is you do it." She dropped the bag, unzipped it. Pulled a hammer and chisel.

"If I don't?" Maria asked, a hand flying immediately to her face because, in all twelve of her years, she'd not asked anything like that, never thought she could.

Aunt Elaine's face fell. "I lied earlier."

"What do you mean?"

"When I said picking a tombstone's your only real choice? It's not. Come." She dropped the tools back in her bag and took Maria's hand in hers. Led her through the cemetery, girl and woman stepping over life after life, every one reduced to a stone marker on a plot of lonely ground.

Near the back of the cemetery, Aunt Elaine stopped. Pointed at a tombstone, newer than the rest. Gleaming in the late afternoon sun.

FACES OF DEATH

Maria squinted, drew closer. Despite the heat, she grew cold, gooseflesh dappling her skin. Her breath caught in her throat. For the life of her, she couldn't understand what her aunt was showing her. What she wanted her to understand. What the true purpose of this whole bizarre errand was.

Not for the first time, Maria wished she'd been born into a normal family. One where they let their children keep their faces.

"See the name?" Aunt Elaine called coldly over her shoulder.

Maria did. *Hector Luna. 1997-2011.*
Unloved.

A dozen different things tumbled for her at once—whispers at family parties, the third set of hash marks above the basement stairs where her parents obsessively charted her and Diego's heights. Her beloved Mr. Fuzzle-Muzzle himself, a hand-me-down her mother said, and then clamped a hand over her mouth and never spoke of where the stuffed bear might've been handed down *from*.

And the look on Aunt Elaine's face when six-year-old Maria worked up the nerve to ask her why she didn't have children of her own—*but I've got* you, *dear*—that spoke of something greater, and weightier, some secret adult reason Maria could never understand.

"Hector, my Hector, thought he could choose."

Maria turned to see Aunt Elaine holding the hammer, low at her side.

"He stood there," she pointed now with the hammer, indicating some barren patch of ground near the rusted gate, "and said no, never, not a chance. Crossed his arms and stomped his feet. So, what did I do?"

Maria's breath hitched, picturing her unknown cousin clear as day, some slapdash amalgamation of aunt and uncle, standing across the cemetery and shouting all the things she wished she could.

"I broke his kneecaps. His arms. Your uncle tattooed his face anyway. We kept him chained to his bed, and whenever he started to heal, however badly, I broke him again." She tapped the hammer against her palm. "Of course, we'd never had to do anything like that before." Her face fell, she absently rubbed at her cheek. "What happens is, you get bedsores. Can't help it. And then sometimes they get infected. So Hector got his way, anyway."

Maria gaped at her, barely comprehending what her aunt was saying. She could do *that?* To her own son?

"Your uncle made me promise I'd not do that again. And I won't. We're not cruel. And you are my favorite niece."

Aunt Elaine took a step towards her, a strange look on her tattooed face. "But so help me, if you don't pick a grave, if you do what Hector did?" She leaned down again, face-to-face with Maria. "I'll bury you with him."

Maria wanted to run, but her body wouldn't listen to the frantic commands issuing forth from her brain. She stared at the hammer—meant for a tombstone of her choice—and wondered how soon the darkness would come if she said no. If she'd wander, like the dead boys and girls Diego spent his nights talking to, recording their stories in black-and-white speckled notebooks.

And if, in her wandering, she'd only end up back at their house, staring into the faces of her brother and mother and father and uncle and aunt—the love they'd had for her gone, replaced by their inescapable duty.

In the end, she picked Soleil Estevez. Seemed as good as any other. Aunt Elaine tap-tap-tapped with the hammer and chisel, sledging off flecks of stone into a vial. Graveyard dust.

Then they went home. In the garage, Uncle Chris cranked heavy metal and mixed the graveyard dust in with his tattoo ink, and then they ate, all of them together at the picnic table in the backyard, elbow to elbow, ladling heaping helpings of barbecue chicken and corn and potato salad onto their plates. Unlike in the car, everyone chattered, mostly about inconsequential things—a new video game Diego was obsessed with, a show her mother watched on NetFlix. Shouldn't they replace the gutters soon?

The adults got a little drunk—Uncle Chris excepted—and Aunt Elaine even gave Maria a tiny glass of wine, child-sized, but she only sipped on it. She didn't like the taste, like grape juice gone bad, but she drank it anyway because her aunt wanted her to. When the warmth pleasantly spread through her cheeks, and everything anyone said sounded a little funnier to her ears, she was glad for it.

Then they led her to the garage and, the whole family circled around, lowered her into a chair, told her to hold very still.

"Let me know if you need a break," Uncle Chris said.

And then it began.

The gun buzzed, the needle descended, and—accompanied by blinding pain—Uncle Chris took away every choice she'd ever have, her whole skeleton-faced family watching, the air thick with cigar smoke and expectation, the beat-up battery-operated boom box on Papa's workbench blasting War, huh, what the fuck is it good for.

Not a once did she scream.

That night the first spirit came to her, a young girl with a slashed throat, a yawning cavity where her left eye should be. Wailing and moaning and writhing in pain unimaginable.

Maria listened to her story, wrote down every anguished syllable.

And then showed her the way home.

Stool Pigeon

So the other weird thing about Bruno Harbeck's bar was he had this pigeon. It sat on a stool next to a vintage Philadelphia Flyers pennant with newspaper layered on the floor underneath to catch the bird shit. Bruno had put this little studded collar around its neck and tethered the thing to an eyebolt sunk in the wall.

As far as I know, the bird didn't have a name. Everybody just called it the pigeon. Or the bird. It didn't really matter. Anybody would've known what you were talking about.

How the health department didn't rain down five kinds of municipal fire and brimstone on Bruno and his bar and his bird, I'll never know. The bird had been there as long as Bruno had. Maybe longer—the pigeon's stool could have marked the site of some long-dead tree where it once perched, before Bruno razed the tree and built the bar up around it.

Maybe first there was the void, and the pigeon was in the void and of the void, and it shat the whole goddamn universe into existence. Somebody's gotta have a myth like that, no? Makes as much sense as an infinitely dense point exploding in a cosmic orgasm, or a geriatric magician whipping up all there is in a mere seven days, or whatever bullshit the

Zoroastrians believe. Something about turtles, maybe? I dunno, I never bothered to look it up.

The other *other* weird thing about Bruno's was your first time there, you had to tell the pigeon a secret before he'd serve you.

Yeah, I'm not kidding. I saw it all the time. In those days, the old neighborhood had become infested with a new generation of suburban thrill-seekers looking to get away from their neatly manicured lawns and participation trophies and discover something real about the world. These hipster kids would walk into Bruno's, beards groomed neat as their parents' lawns, with plug earrings and T-shirts bearing the names of bands no one's ever heard of, and order a PBR. Bruno would say nope, you gotta tell the bird a secret first. They'd say what, huh, repeat that?

And Bruno would. They'd balk, ask each other a series of half questions ("You mean—" "You can't be—" "Oh, honey, I think he is") but finally, they'd march up to the bird, lean down, and whisper in its ear.

Sometimes Bruno, who was usually leaning on the bar, the sports page spread out in front of him, would stand bolt upright and say, "That wasn't a secret."

The kid would play dumb. But Bruno would just say, "I can tell. There's this thing he does. And what you just told him wasn't no fucking secret."

The kid would argue, hem and haw, but eventually he'd lean down and whisper something else to the bird. And Bruno would just say, "See? That wasn't so hard, now was it?"

I never got tired of watching, and I'd been watching for a very long time. I spent more time at Bruno's than I did at home, where all I had to do was

STOOL PIGEON

fiddle with the rabbit ears until something I didn't want to watch anyway came on TV. And I couldn't go very many places. Back in '97, I'd been in a car accident, a bad one. My right leg hadn't healed right, screamed in displeasure if I spent too much time on it, and looked like a peg leg carved by a blind, drunk carpenter who'd maybe heard of prostheses but hadn't seen the real McCoy up close. Luckily, Bruno's lay mere blocks away.

The secret I told the bird was about the accident.

I was on disability, since before the accident I worked construction, and I sure wasn't good for that anymore. I wasn't good for much if I'm giving a full accounting of myself here. I woke most days, got cleaned up, and limped on down to Bruno's. There I sat, drinking ginger ale by the gallon and watching Bruno read the sports page and feeling his bird stare at me with eyes like chunks of obsidian. Bruno's was one of those places where most everybody knew everybody, except of course for those college kids who'd stop in occasionally—we jokingly called them foreigners. It wasn't a bad place to spend my time.

Except for the five o'clock hour, when Clarence came in.

Clarence was a big fat guy with a jovial smile who worked in a pastry factory, made knockoff Hostess pies and hot buns, so he always reeked of dough and icing. That wasn't so bad. The real reason I didn't like him was because I knew the secret he whispered to the pigeon.

It wasn't his secret. It was mine.

I guess the bird didn't care if you told a secret it had heard before or a secret that wasn't yours to tell. As long as it was an actual secret, that was good enough for the bird, and therefore good enough for Bruno.

I should have known things couldn't go on like that.

So one day, there I was in Bruno's, ginger ale on a soggy napkin in front of me, dangling my bum leg off the stool, when the clock ticked five-ish and Clarence walked in. Bruno looked up from the sports page long enough to grunt. A few other drunks said hi—Bruno's was unusually crowded that day with lushes who'd given up a secret to the bird.

The only open seat was next to me.

Clarence turned his bulk and eased down the walkway between the barstools and the scattered tables, laying a thick, callused hand on the bar next to me. Dried frosting spackled his knuckle hair.

"Hey, man," he said, "this seat taken?"

I shrugged, because what else could I do? I wanted to get up and walk away, but my leg doesn't lend itself to hasty or dignified exits.

"Helluva day," Clarence said, sitting down heavily on the stool, fetid air whooshing out from the cushion's torn seams. Bruno poured him a frosty mug of Coors.

"Hey," Bruno said.

"Hey," Clarence said back. You don't go to Bruno's for the conversation.

Bruno went back to his paper. Clarence stirred the foam topping his beer with a finger. I drank my ginger ale. Everybody else minded their own beeswax. The pigeon stared us all down.

STOOL PIGEON

"So how you been?" Clarence asked.

I didn't reply, like one of those movies where somebody says something and the other person doesn't say shit, and you're screaming at the TV for them to reply, and it's annoying. I clearly heard him. I could've told him fine or fuck off. I didn't do either. Just sat there, pissed.

Like I said, I'm not good for much these days.

Clarence and I used to be friends. Not great friends, like we'd help each other move or something, but the kind of friends that nodded to each other and shot the shit and then didn't exist until the next time we were six beers deep at the same bar. Those kind of friends. The kind who sometimes, after a few drinks, you tell things you shouldn't.

This was all before Bruno's, at this other place we used to go. We got too drunk one night, and I told him the secret I'd eventually tell the bird. The next day, sobered up, the mistakes of the night before still ringing in my head, I quit drinking. Funny how I get in an accident, wreck my life and more, and that doesn't make me quit, but the night I have one too many and tell somebody else about that accident? Plug meet jug.

I hadn't touched a drop since.

But I still liked bars, with their familiar faces and smells and low buzzing conversation, which was what brought me to Bruno's. I found it easier not to drink in a bar I'd never been drunk in. But then Clarence heard I was going to Bruno's, followed me over. And when Bruno said to do the thing with the bird? Clarence told the pigeon *my* fucking secret.

I could tell because when Clarence's lips moved, that bird and its glassy eyes looked me dead in the face and didn't turn away until Clarence was done.

"Not talking to me, huh?" Clarence said. "I don't get it, man. You stop talking to me, stop drinking, all on the same day. I been letting it go, but—"

"So keep letting it go," I said.

Clarence shook his head. "Nah, man. I don't know what I did, but I don't like walking around feeling like we ain't right. So what the fuck did I say to you that night? I know I didn't grab your dick or nothing, that ain't me."

I took a sip of ginger ale. Swished it around in my mouth, wishing it was beer. A talk like this was made for beer. I didn't have any beer, so I didn't talk.

"And man, when you told me that shit about the accident, I didn't judge you, I just—"

"Like I said, let it go. That was years ago."

Clarence shrugged. "Fine. Be that way. You want to be an asshole, be an asshole. My conscience is clean now."

A grey-haired lady at the end of the bar got up and shuffled toward the door. I glanced down at my leg, wondering if a move was worth the pain.

"Don't worry about it." Clarence grabbed his beer and went to take the empty seat.

Abruptly he spun around and walked back to me.

"At least tell the bird," he said.

"What?" I asked.

"Tell the bird why you've been so pissed at me all these years."

I shook my head. "Forget it. I told the bird a secret already."

"So tell it another one."

"That's not how it works," I said. "Hey, Bruno, tell Clarence this ain't how it works."

STOOL PIGEON

"It ain't how it works," Bruno said, smoothing out the newspaper in front of him.

Clarence looked at me, moisture pooling in the corners of his eyes. Was he really going to *cry*? The thought disgusted me. The idea that another human being would be so preoccupied with my company made my skin crawl. Why would I matter so much?

He opened his mouth to say something, but I was already lowering my good leg to the ground. I pushed off the stool. A twinge of pain radiated up and down my bad leg. Leaning on my cane, I shuffled over to the pigeon.

The bird sat on its stool, fat with secrets, the corner stinking of shit. It regarded me with blank eyes. Gave its wings a little stutter in a parody of a shrug.

At least the pigeon wasn't going all moony over me, too.

Clarence's eyes bored into my back as I leaned down and told the bird, in the quietest voice I could, why I couldn't stand his ass.

"Bullshit," Bruno called. I looked up and caught him glaring at me.

"What?" I said.

"You didn't tell him the real reason."

Clarence's bottom lip quivered. "You serious? Can't even tell the *bird* what your problem is with me?" He turned to the rest of the room. "This guy won't even tell the bird why he don't like me."

Bruno's being Bruno's, nobody seemed to notice.

I leaned heavily on my cane, wondering how the hell a sober man gets himself into situations like this. "I told him. Scout's honor." I held up two fingers in a half-remembered salute from my boyhood. I didn't think it was right.

Bruno shook his head. "How long you been coming here? How many people you see try to lie to the bird? And every time, every single damn time, I call them on it. There's a thing he does. If it's not a real secret, I can tell. And you didn't tell him no fucking secret."

"You know what?" I said. "Screw both of you."

I limped back over to my stool, avoiding Clarence's gaze. Bruno stared daggers at me. As I began the complicated process of sitting back down, Bruno marched over and snatched my drink away.

"What the hell?"

"You know the rules. I can't serve you till you tell the bird a secret."

"I already did! Years ago!"

Bruno dumped my glass in the sink behind the bar. "Yeah, you did. But then you lied, so the first one don't count no more."

"Bruno—" I began, but he turned his back on me and looked down at the sports page, the subject permanently closed. Clarence shook his head and took a seat at the far end of the bar.

I sat there, half on the stool, half off, feeling like I'd somehow broken through to a brand-new rock bottom never before glimpsed in the million relapses of a million drunks. The worst part was I *had* told the bird a true secret. Clarence told the bird my secret, and that's why I couldn't stand him.

Or so I thought.

Waves of laughter overtook me, spasms of hilarity that made me clutch the bar for dear life. I felt like a Magellan, sailing a sea of rough absurdity no explorer had ever imagined. A line of faces turned, appraised me for a moment, probably hoping I'd fall, then went back to their drinks. I couldn't stop laughing, and the hint of tears I'd seen in Clarence's eyes a moment before became reality in mine.

Accompanied by the sound of my own manic laughter, and careful not to put too much weight on my bad leg, I slowly trudged across Bruno's to the door and showed myself out.

Days passed, as they do. I didn't go back to Bruno's. I hung around my apartment, tidying up the place, finally hanging up this picture of a sailboat I'd bought at a flea market years before. Going through boxes of old papers, bills and such, even throwing some out.

There were two other bars within walking distance. Well, walking distance for a cripple—an able-bodied man would've had more options. I tried one, then the other. Neither seemed amenable to letting me occupy a stool for hours, drinking nothing stronger than ginger ale. I was used to apathetic gazes and silent nods. Now I got dirty looks and open hostility.

So, I fell off the wagon. Fell all kinds of other places, too. A drunk's greatest asset is his two legs. I had one and a half. When I made it home with only torn pants, I'd call the night a success.

I started tacking a taxi ride onto the end of my nights so I'd only have to fall down the stairs to my basement apartment instead of up and down four blocks of sidewalk. The taxis strained my disability checks. Payday loans and my landlord's religiosity filled the gap—Jesus wouldn't allow him to just kick out a cripple. What you do to the least of these, right?

Some nights I'd scream awake thinking about those glowing neon signs promising quick cash, and the stoop-shouldered people, eyes blank like Bruno's pigeon, queuing up in front of a bulletproof glass kiosk and begging to pay them Tuesday for a hamburger today.

This couldn't last.

I started early at one of the other bars, couldn't tell you which one. Treated myself to a glass of cognac first, since I was celebrating. The bartender asked me what for.

"I'm going home," I told him.

Cheaper stuff followed, and a lot of it. By the time I wore out my welcome, I only had a few bucks left in my pocket. Enough for a ginger ale, even a tip for Bruno. Seemed like a sign.

The walk passed in a flash, and I staggered into Bruno's sometime in the middle of the afternoon. Bruno looked up from his sports page and glared at me.

"You know the rules," he said.

I nodded, feeling much like a bobblehead doll. "Yeah, I know the rules," I slurred. "I'll tell the damn bird what it wants to know."

Ignoring the handful of regulars gaping at my return, I stumbled over to the stool, where the bird sat regarding me with those impassive eyes. Those maddening eyes. All the secrets of the world, or at least the tiny world Bruno and Clarence and I lived in, hidden behind those eyes—forever trapped.

I leaned down and whispered to the bird. I

STOOL PIGEON

thought I'd told it the truth last time. Or at least the truth as I'd understood it, but that wasn't enough, there had to be some other truth hiding in my own mind.

Tongue loosened by an afternoon of self-abuse, I spilled my guts to the pigeon. The accident, which I'd been mostly sober for, and what I'd told Clarence about when I'd been drunk. How they figured I just nodded off after a long day at a job site. And then everything after, including why I was back and finally trying to tell the best truth I could, and then I hit on it—the real reason I'd been so mad at Clarence, all these years. Not because he told the bird my secret. Because I told *him* my secret, and he never thought less of me on account of what I did. Still wanted to be my fucking friend after that. What kind of a person's okay with something like that?

When I was done, I stood there panting, leaning heavily on my cane, not a secret left in me. Hoping the bird would accept it. Those blank eyes told me nothing.

The pigeon twisted its head around to peck at its tail feathers. I turned around too. Bruno put a glass of ginger ale down on the bar.

"This one's on the house," he said, and went back to his sports page.

Around five, Clarence came in, the sweat stains on his white T-shirt glowing in the low light of the bar. He nodded when he saw me, and he looked from me to the bird and back again. Saying nothing, he sat down at the end of the bar and ordered his usual Coors.

With a shot of whiskey on the side.

Maybe I should have told him how I spilled my

beans to the bird, but it didn't occur to me—I was back, Bruno was serving me—he could do the math. And I guess I figured if I told him I told the bird, he wouldn't leave it at that. Maybe for an hour, two, a night or a week, but we'd be buddy-buddy again and he'd be asking me questions and maybe one day I'd spill the real reason I didn't want Clarence anywhere near me, which was for me and the bird and no one else.

Over the next hour, I drank ginger ale and got head-achingly sober. Clarence went the other way. It felt good to be back in Bruno's, but Clarence made me nervous. He was drinking to get drunk. Maybe psyching himself up for something. Nobody else seemed to notice. Maybe because they were doing the same thing. It was a bar, after all.

My head ached harder. Bruno read his sports page and refilled drinks. The bird pecked at its feathers. Clarence started to sway.

I didn't like it.

He rose from his stool, knocking it over. A few heads turned at the clatter. Bruno even looked up from his newspaper.

"Clarence? You okay?"

Clarence shook his head, hid his face with his hands. I looked down at the bubbles in my glass, the melting ice. Whatever was going on with him, I wanted no part of it. Just as I'd wanted no part of him since the night I'd drunkenly told him about the accident.

Clarence rushed me. I gripped the handle of my cane, hoping to get one good shot in before he took me apart, but then he was past me with a faint pastry stink, standing in front of the bird's stool, tears streaming down his cheeks.

Stool Pigeon

"Tell me. I want to know."

"Clarence," Bruno said, "I think you've had a bit too much."

"Tell me," Clarence repeated. "Tell me, tell me, tell me."

"That's enough. I want you outta here."

"Tell me," Clarence said, snatching the bird off its stool and raising it level with his teary eyes. The bird wriggled in his grasp, pecked at his fingers.

"Clarence!" Bruno thundered. "Put the fucking bird down now. I won't tell you again."

The whole bar held their breath, stared at the big, blubbering man and the helpless pigeon in his grasp. Nobody had ever touched the bird before. My stomach, even leveled by the ginger ale I'd been dosing with ever since I earned my way back into Bruno's, slumped sick and hollow beneath my rib cage.

I hadn't felt like this since the accident, since those last, slow-motion moments when I'd screamed "fuck this," taken my hands off the wheel, and drifted over into oncoming traffic, where my truck violently greeted a '94 Toyota Tercel driven by a sixteen-year-old kid who'd never get to turn seventeen.

The worst part was the split second when my eyes adjusted to the oncoming headlights, and I saw how small that car was, how wide the kid's eyes were, his dirty smudge of a goatee, the strawberry air freshener hanging from the rearview, and the silent scream on his lips.

No. The worst part was knowing that kid got the gift I'd been trying to give myself.

Chik-chak.

We all looked at Bruno aiming a sawed-off. "Goddamn you, Clarence."

A violent boom rent the air. Something wet spattered my cheek. Clarence wavered on his heels, the remains of his face a ragged mess of torn flesh and scoured cheekbones. The rest of it covered the Flyers pennant.

His hands spasmed, the pigeon's bones cracking as Clarence's knees gave way, and he tumbled to the floor to finish up his dying on the layered newspaper streaked with bird shit.

Bruno stood there, chest heaving, shotgun still pointed at the wall covered in Clarence's blood and brains and skin and that damn Flyers pennant. A bright white skull fragment stuck right there in the bull's-eye center of the *P*. Down among the bird shit, Clarence's body twitched.

Nobody moved. Nobody said anything. Finally, somebody coughed. Mighta been me.

Bruno gently lowered the shotgun and sat it on the bar. He took a dirty towel and held it to his face, a stifled moan emanating from beneath. Ice cubes tinkled in rocks glasses as the other patrons brought drinks to their lips, diving headlong into the familiar and sane.

Bruno walked around the bar and leaned on the stool his bird had stood on all those years, since maybe before there'd been a bar, even. He looked down at Clarence, and the bird. Sobbing, he squatted and gently pulled the pigeon from Clarence's meaty dead fingers.

All around the bar, people finished their drinks and ran for the exits. Somebody would call the police. Or maybe somebody in the apartment upstairs already had.

I spun my stool around, clambered off, trying my

best to ignore the snuffling sounds coming from the floor behind me. Limping to the exit, my throat dry, twinges of pain shooting up my bum leg. Knowing I'd just watched my secret die twice in a span of seconds.

As I pushed the front door open, wailing sirens echoing through the night, that kid's face came to me again. The silent scream, and how it should have been mine, if it hadn't been so dark, if I hadn't been in such a hurry to get the hell off the planet, I couldn't tell a compact from a semi.

And I saw Clarence, too, sitting in the passenger seat next to the kid, lit up by my high beams. What formed on his face was not a scream, silent or otherwise, but a question, whose answer could now only be found in the brain of a dead pigeon clutched tightly to its broken owner's chest, and the mind of a bent and crooked man who honestly didn't give a shit.

MOONBOY

"Moon, moon! golden horns! Melt the bullet, blunt the knife, rot the cudgel, strike fear into man, beast, and reptile, so that they may not . . . tear from him his warm hide"
—Ralston, *The Songs of the Russian People*

DRAGGING A BODY through the woods was a damn sight harder than it looked in the movies. Especially a living one. At first, Teddy threw the gas station clerk over his shoulder, but the kid was too heavy to carry more than a few feet at a time, even though he was short and skinny, barely looked old enough to buy beer. Plus, he was kicking like a sonofabitch. Teddy'd wrapped the kid's ankles and wrists in duct tape, so the kicking wasn't really kicking *per se*, just a lame, ineffectual toe-tap, but it sure didn't make things easier.

So now, Teddy was dragging the clerk by his taped-up ankles. Hardly better—the kid was pure dead weight, and still wriggling like a nightcrawler on a hook. Teddy figured this must be how pack animals felt, if a plow or carriage decided to fight back. He grunted, sweat beading on his brow, kept muscling the kid down the tiny path through the trees he'd worn over years of visiting his special place.

MOONBOY

The kid's head banged heavily against a rock, and his eyes rolled back.

"Damn it, watch with that squirmin', would you? You're gonna bash your brains in before we even get there."

Frantic, muffled sounds came from the clerk's duct-taped mouth, which Teddy figured to be screaming. He sighed, kicking himself—he'd gone and frightened the kid even more than he already had, what with the kidnapping and the restraints and now the whole dark-lonesome-murder-woods thing.

"Oh man, I realize how that sounded," Teddy said, patting the boy's shin. "Poor choice of words. When we get where we're going, no bashing. Scout's honor." He held up three fingers in the Boy Scout salute— muscle memory from once upon a time.

A murmur of what could have been relief, disbelief, or a bit of both came through the duct tape. Teddy resumed his dragging, careful to watch for rocks in the path. If he spotted one, he'd try to go around it, spare the clerk some pain. But it was getting harder to see the trail with the sun rapidly setting, and he couldn't hold a flashlight and drag the kid at the same time. He knew the trail well enough, but he'd never had to worry about rocks before.

His companion had a name, but Teddy didn't know what it was. When he'd asked the clerk to check his oil at the gas station earlier that afternoon, he made sure not to let his eyes wander to the kid's nametag. The request got the kid out to Teddy's car, a tire iron and a roll of duct tape did the rest. Once the kid was all trussed up in the trunk, half-conscious body curled up like a puppy over the spare tie, Teddy ripped the name tag off his shirt, just so's he wouldn't accidentally get a look later. Then he hit the road. Caught a cop car pull into the station in his rearview, right before he rounded the bend.

Took that close call for a sign—the moon was looking out for him. She *wanted* this. Teddy gave the kid's name tag a little kiss for further good luck before he tossed it out the window somewhere near Tuckerton.

A few miles after that, they were pulling up to the woods, and the path to Teddy's special place.

Now here they were, struggling down a trail. Teddy's arms burned with exertion, his soaked t-shirt stuck to his back. The kid wasn't struggling as much, though. Maybe he'd convinced himself some weird stuff was about to happen, but afterward, Teddy would let him go.

Of course he was wrong.

Teddy felt bad about killing the kid, but what else was he supposed to do? He'd tried everything he could think of—cooked up an ointment of henbane, silverweed, bat's blood, and soot, rubbed it all over his body, but that just made him all greasy and smelly. Reciting the gypsy curse he found on some Wiccan website made him feel stupid, and he shat his brains out for the rest of the day when, after a fresh rain, he drank from what he *thought* was a wolf's paw print.

"Almost there," Teddy said, as much to his fatigued muscles as to the gas station clerk.

The sun was almost down, and they were nearly to his special place. He'd timed it almost perfectly, just like with the cop at the gas station. Maybe that was another good sign.

Except his arms were completely dead.

Teddy dropped the kid's feet, allowed them a

MOONBOY

quick break. Just a few minutes wouldn't hurt, would it? Since they were so close and all.

He leaned back against a tree, wiping his brow with the hem of his shirt. Wished he'd thought of some other, easier way to get the clerk out there. When he planned it all out, he thought about bringing his mother's old wheelchair, still folded up in the hallway closet. But no, the trail wasn't nearly wide enough, and he couldn't imagine the little rubber wheels doing well in this terrain.

"Mmmph!"

The kid looked up at him with shiny, fearful eyes that still had a sliver of hope in them. His face was wet with tears and sweat, streaked with soil. His uniform was similarly covered in dirt and twigs. Some errant branch or rock had ripped a good-sized gash in the sleeve of his polo shirt.

"Sorry about your shirt," Teddy muttered. Then he grabbed the boy's ankles again and pulled him along.

They didn't have to go far. Soon, the ground rose slightly beneath his feet. Teddy's heart beat faster, a weird tickle ran up his insides. The rest of him was sweating like a bastard, and now his palms were too because guess what?

"We're here," Teddy said softly, like a moan.

The kid whimpered through his duct tape.

A break in the treeline up ahead marked the place where everything was about to change. With a grunt, he pulled the gas station attendant the last few feet and into the clearing. He paused for a moment, breathing heavily, hands on his knees. He was dimly aware of the boy rolling around in the dirt beside him. Trying to do . . . something.

After his breath evened out he looked around with a grin, taking in his special place. It wasn't big, irregularly shaped and fifteen feet across at its widest point, but you could see the moon, which was the main thing Teddy cared about. The ground continued to rise to the center, where a few large rocks clustered together like children sharing secrets at recess. The trees growing directly around the clearing were a bit shorter than the others they'd passed on the way in. Younger. Teddy thought maybe at one time, long ago, the clearing was just a bit bigger, and over time the forest had taken back a little of what belonged to it. But now it was just the right size for him.

The moon poked out above the tree line, and crickets chirped from somewhere in the surrounding woods. There wasn't a cloud in the dark sky.

"Nice night, huh?" Teddy said.

Not even a muffled response. The boy had gone catatonic, now that they'd reached their destination.

Teddy's special place was his special place just because, but it was also where he lost his virginity. He found it on a hunting trip with his cousin Thad, the one his mother used to say was no good. They'd been pumping off rounds at nothing at all when they came across it. The rocks seemed a fine place to smoke a joint, kick their feet up for a bit. Nice and peaceful, with the fluffy white clouds above and the wind lightly rustling through the ring of trees, but otherwise unremarkable.

But that night, Teddy had a dream. A faceless woman in white led him through the same forest he'd walked with Thad, and every time a branch scratched his flesh it was like sharp nails caressing his skin. His loins were burning when they emerged from the trees and into the clearing, a full moon blazing above.

MOONBOY

And in the sight of God and the moon and the Goddess of the Moon, she'd mounted him and rode the fire right out of him.

Afterward, she reached out to caress his cheek, silhouetted in the moonlight. But just before her hand brushed against his skin, she whirled and ran off into the trees. On more legs than two.

Teddy woke from that dream knowing it was much more—a message, sent by the moon. All that could be his. The woman, the beast she became? She was real.

And she was waiting.

He went back to the woods weekly, sometimes more. Started pawning his mother off on a relative for the night so he could stalk around the clearing stark-naked from dusk till dawn, beating his chest and howling pathetic howls, poor imitations of what he thought a wolf might sound like. Other nights he'd just sit there, cross-legged, like a kindergartener waiting for his teacher to tell him what to do next. But he never saw the faceless woman, or the thing she became after she ran off into the night.

Why he knew he had to change.

And now, finally, he was going to do it.

The hairs on the back of Teddy's neck stood on end. He couldn't stop smiling. This was it, this was really it. After all the dumb tricks he'd tried to turn wolf, all the wretched nights alone, whimpering in his bed, he'd hit on a humdinger of an idea. Cut out the middleman, appeal right to the moon herself. With the boy's blood to sweeten the deal, Teddy figured she couldn't say no.

He stretched his arms and pulled the boy along for the final time, right to the middle of the clearing. Dog prints littered the ground, along with a big patch of freshly-turned earth a few feet away. It wasn't a wolf per se, but Teddy figured the Liebermann's husky was close enough. The thing looked like a wolf to him.

He looked up at the moon and winked, giving her a little wave. "Okay, hope you're paying attention. Have I got a show for you!"

Teddy flipped the boy over and straddled his back, ignoring his muffled whining. Duct tape really was the greatest invention known to man. Not only did it keep the clerk's hands and feet right where he wanted them, but it also kept him quiet, too.

He slid a bowl underneath the kid's throat—a dog bowl that once belonged to the Liebermann's husky—to catch the spillage and pulled the hunting knife from its sheath at his belt. Teddy took a long breath, looked up at the moon one more time, and started to cut.

He thought he could do it in one long, clean stroke, but his first jab barely broke the skin. Taking a fistful of the kid's hair, he twisted the knife around, digging it in deeper. The kid bucked underneath him, but Teddy hung on like a rodeo ace. He had a good fifty pounds on the clerk.

With jerking, sawing motions, Teddy brought the knife across the kid's throat, giving him a brand-new smile from ear to ear. Tossing the knife to the side, he repositioned the bowl and tried to keep the kid as still as he could. Waste not, want not.

It took forever, but the clerk finally stopped jerking around. Blood still streamed from his neck, but the bowl was nearly full. Teddy carefully pulled it out from under the kid and set it on one of the big rocks. Then he grabbed the corpse by the ankles and dragged it back to the tree line, not meeting its blank

MOONBOY

gaze with the same assiduousness with which he'd earlier avoided looking at its name tag. He left the body slumped haphazardly by the trees.

With any luck, it would make a good snack for later.

Back in the center of the clearing, he stripped off his clothes, half-hard already. He wondered if she'd come for him right away, or if he'd have to catch her scent and chase her through the night. Either way, he'd find her, and then they could run and screw and kill and sing praises to the moon for all time.

He dipped his fingers into the bowl, painted symbols on his chest, arcane emblems he'd discovered in his research. Runes of transformation, runes of supplication. Ancient images that screamed at the moon louder than his voice ever could. The iron scent of blood filled his nostrils, and he began to salivate.

What blood was left in the bowl, he poured into the tracks he'd created with the husky's paws. Dropping to all fours, he glanced at the moon one last time to make sure she was paying attention, a cloud hadn't wandered by to obscure her view. The moon watched him from on high, full and bright and utterly indifferent. Not for long, he hoped.

He lapped the gas station attendant's blood from the paw prints, the iron tang curling his tongue. He made sure he got every drop, suppressing a gag as dirt wormed its way into his mouth. Teddy pawed away the grit, turned his head and spat.

And then he looked up at the moon and howled—loud and long as he could, and damned if they weren't real howls. Not the childish little play-yelps he'd reeled off on half-a-hundred occasions out here in his special place, but real, honest-to-goodness, freeze-your-blood-in-your-veins howls.

The moon sure as hell had to hear that.

He paused there, on hands and knees, waiting, listening. He already had the voice. Maybe she'd come to him now, and her kiss would take him the rest of the way. His cock throbbed between his legs. He howled once more, longer and louder than ever before, calling the faceless woman to him.

Something moved in the woods. Leaves rustled, branches snapped. Teddy spun his head around, trying to locate the sound. Where was she?

"Playing coy, my love?" he said with a laugh. "I'm right here, come to daddy!"

Lights flashed through the clearing, pinning him in their beams. He snarled, squinting, barely discerning dark shapes ringing the clearing.

"Police! Don't you move!" a voice yelled, followed by the distinctive chik-chak of a racking shotgun.

"Hey, are you—what the hell!" another voice shouted.

Teddy squatted on all fours, eyes burning in the beams. One final challenge, maybe? A test to prove him worthy of her love, worthy of the moon?

Drool dripped from the corners of his mouth, a guttural roar forming in his throat. And then he sprang off his back heels and charged at the lights, at the men behind them, his mind if not his body gone fully lupine.

And then he was lying on his back, body filled with bullets and buckshot, staring up at the moon. And as the night drew close around him, the pale indifferent bitch whispered a single word in his rounded-off ears.

No.

PRESERVATION

1.

THE MAN SEATED across from Moston certainly looked like a killer—hulking, heavy-browed, a jagged scar running from cheek to stubbly chin, the sleeves of his army jacket pushed up to reveal tightly-muscled, hairy forearms thick with compressed power, unsubtly intimating a grip that could crush bone.

But most of all, the dark look in his deep-set eyes spoke in no uncertain terms of what he'd done, what he could do, and how he felt about it. Not for the first time, Moston questioned the wisdom of inviting a man like Argo Gabrogian into his home.

But wisdom had long been in short supply in Moston's household, or he wouldn't have had a reason to associate with the likes of Gabrogian in the first place.

"What is the nature of the—" Gabrogian paused, sipping almost daintily from the teacup in his calloused hand, "—entity?"

His tone was flat, bordering on disinterested. The fellow who'd come to rid Moston of his roach problem two weeks before had seemed more intrigued.

They sat on respective leather couches in the drawing room of Moston's townhouse, a once well-appointed three-story affair. Now, much of the furniture was draped in sheets, dust and cobwebs collecting in ceiling corners, the faint reek of mildew omnipresent. Upkeep of the household usually fell to Moston, but since Annelina's disappearance he'd lacked the impetus to do much more than the bare minimum. Floors went unswept, dishes piled up in the kitchen sink, burnt-out bulbs sat dead in their sockets.

"The nature," Gabrogian prompted.

Moston worried at the handle of his own teacup—their second-finest set—but didn't raise it to his lips. "I suppose," he finally said, "no one knows for sure. The city's awash with whispers, always has been. No one acknowledges what's happening outright, but—" he swallowed hard, already feeling like he'd made a huge mistake. Confused himself, a weak and pampered probable-widower, for an avenger.

The fact he'd hired Gabrogian, or was about to, instead of buying a pistol and taking to the alleys with his collar turned up and a black hat pulled low on his brow, should've been his first clue.

"Tell me of these whispers," Gabrogian said patiently. "Whatever you know of this thing called Volscher. Starting with the name. What does it mean?"

Moston blanched at the mere mention of Volscher—everyone knew it, no one said it—and shook his head quickly. "It's just—his name, I suppose. Everyone knows."

Gabrogian set his teacup down gently on its saucer. "Philosophers of antiquity believed everything in this world had something called a quiddity. An inherent essence, making it what it is. When does a pebble become a stone?" He fixed Moston with a hard

PRESERVATION

look. "Some things, we see them and know them for what they are. Go on."

Moston blinked, stunned by the unexpected erudition, then tried to pick up where he left off. "There's abandoned places, all around the city. Places he's claimed. You can tell because of his sigil—a bisected figure eight. Sometimes it's scribbled on an alley wall, or etched in wet cement. They're hard to see, but they're there. If you're in one of those places—" Moston shivered, "—have a care. There's rules."

"What rules?"

"These places—they're not to be disturbed. In any way."

"How so?"

Moston shrugged. "Anything, really. That's the problem. Graffiti. Breaking windows. Picking up litter. It's impossible to tell what might raise his ire. Best to avoid them altogether, but like I said, the sigil is small and easy to miss. Sometimes you don't realize you're in a *protected area*—" he swallowed hard, the phrase strange on his tongue, "—until it's too late."

"And when someone disturbs one of these places?"

"They disappear. Never to be seen again."

"Mm." Gabrogian looked away, let his gaze wander around the room. Moston hoped his guest wasn't thinking about simply snapping his neck and robbing him blind instead of completing their business. Then again, Moston's connections assured him Gabrogian was discreet, and consummately professional. He'd evidently completed similar transactions in places as far-flung as Colleville, Perricott City, and Toretto, and left his employers quite pleased with his work.

And alive.

Gabrogian finally looked back at Moston—which did nothing to reassure him of his guest's intentions. "Why?"

"Why what?"

"Why do you care?"

Moston indicated the room around them, everything but the couches and the coffee table draped, the rest of the house silent, unlived-in. Opened his mouth to try to offer something, to somehow sum up what had been taken from him by a whisper, a rumor—

Gabrogian waved dismissively. "How do I find this entity?"

"Are you familiar with the south bridge over the Steelhead River?"

Gabrogian grunted.

Moston wasn't sure what he meant, so continued, "Head west for a few miles down Elscolm Avenue until you reach the river. There's a broken train trestle. One of his places. Desecrate it, and he will come."

Gabrogian nodded slowly. Asked no further questions, made no move to leave.

"Oh," Moston said softly. He pulled a thick envelope from his jacket pocket and slid it across the table.

Gabrogian laid a palm over the envelope and drew it to him. "This is what you want?"

Moston nodded his head so vigorously his glasses slid down his long and thin nose. "Yes."

"Then it's done." Gabrogian stood quickly, slipping the envelope into the pocket of his army jacket, and left the room before it even occurred to Moston to show his guest out.

PRESERVATION

II.

Though he could not remember where he'd read it—long ago, surely, back when books held some appeal for him, along with all the other things of the world—Moston recalled a quote, something about the inherent insanity of cities. On a fundamental level, civilization was almost nonsensical, its incongruity accepted, and unquestioned, lest every last denizen fall screaming headlong into madness.

Given the reality of his own metropolis, Moston had to agree.

Volscher had long been regarded by the citizenry—albeit in unspoken terms—as an inconvenient but immutable aspect of the environment in which they lived, not unlike the way a resident of a tropical region might view a monsoon. Everyone was aware of the thing in their midst, even if they didn't talk about it. Some dismissed Volscher as an urban legend (of whom a small minority were violently disabused of their notions every year). Others believed without *believing*, taking care to avoid parts of town rumored to be rife with areas to which he'd laid claim. Easy enough, as these were places no one wanted to go anyway—a burned-out shell of a building, a cracked and broken dead-end street, a warehouse with a collapsing roof. Better to leave such places alone, to allow Volscher, through sigils and secret diktats and vanishings, to "preserve" them; or, more precisely, the state of entropy they enjoyed.

Then there were the zealots—small and unconnected pockets of souls throughout the city who supposedly worshiped him. For Volscher had been with the city since its inception, or at least since the first new building lapsed into a state of disrepair. Something of his rumored characteristics suggested at once a man, a ghost, and a god, a trinity which added up to none of the above. A contrarian object of worship.

Moston never gave the matter much thought. If he did happen to find himself in an unfamiliar place, he simply observed the vague rules as he understood them, like a seasoned traveler adapting to local customs, and soon enough found himself home.

Annelina did not believe, on any level. Analytical Annelina, skeptical of anything that did not fit into her neatly ordered view of the universe. Moston found it refreshing when they'd first been introduced—the women he'd dated previously all had a taste for the esoteric and arcane, obsessed with everything from astrology to witchcraft. Annelina rarely acknowledged what she could not see, touch or taste, a naturalist through and through. Early in their relationship, Moston asked her whether she believed in God. She answered with a brusque "of course not" and then asked if he was going to finish his linguine.

But to his unending sorrow, belief in the fantastic is not a prerequisite for it to devour you.

On a cool November night the previous year, Annelina called Moston to rant about a particularly inept city inspector—apparently they'd been scheduled to meet at the site of her latest construction project, but the woman hadn't shown up. Not an unusual circumstance; Annelina worked herself into rages whenever her exacting standards were not met, and any attempt at placation would result in her ire

PRESERVATION

being redirected Moston's way. So instead he employed inoffensive and vaguely supportive interjections ("yes, yes," "that is ridiculous," "unbelievable") while letting her vent. He didn't mind, her passion was one of the qualities he found most captivating.

Just as her tirade reached a fever pitch, her voice cut out. Moston looked at the display—they were still connected. "Hello, hello," he asked, over and over.

But there was no reply.

He ended the call and tried her again—voicemail. He paced the floors of their house, and when the hour of her arrival came and went he called the police.

The following weeks were difficult. The authorities did not take Moston seriously at first, and when they did they assumed he was connected to her disappearance. The shroud of suspicion cast over Moston left him alone, adrift. Friends and neighbors dropped by to comfort him, but all were awkward and stiff and did not stay very long. Eventually, the police determined through cellular records that Moston and Annelina had been in different sectors of the city the night she disappeared, and quietly recalibrated their investigation to focus on her business relationships.

But the damage to Moston's reputation was done, and the thought of going on without her, for the remaining thirty or forty years he might live, seemed impossible. When the police investigation stalled, Moston began his own.

Through subtle applications of the fortune they shared, Moston determined his wife's last known location: a broken train trestle overlooking the Steelhead River. Moston knew the area well— Annelina's firm bought it for a song, with a plan to build river-view condos. When she'd breezed into their townhouse after the deal closed, giddy with the prospect of turning a vacant lot into prime waterfront real estate, Moston tried his best to share her elation, but could not. Anxiety gripped him—what if that broken trestle was *His?*

But he said nothing.

After she disappeared, he took a taxi there to see the place for himself, hoping he could intuit some clue as to his wife's fate.

When he saw the broken figure eight scored into rusted iron, he knew Annelina was gone to places from which the authorities would never recover her.

Moston swore there, on that riverbank—silently, for fear of bringing Volscher down upon himself—he would use every last penny of their fortune to find out whether gods or ghosts or things beyond definition could bleed.

III.

Argo Gabrogian left the townhouse and handed Moston's envelope to the first vagrant he passed. He always asked his clients for money—and a substantial sum at that—to prove they were serious. He never kept it. Gabrogian's physical needs were few and well provided for by his military pension. His sole spiritual need was the work, of which there was no shortage, and so he walked the world, content.

He patted his side to ensure his tool was at the ready, more habit than confirmation. Touching the subtle bulge under his coat calmed him, helped him focus.

Although Argo Gabrogian was far from an anxious sort.

PRESERVATION

He headed down Elscolm Avenue, eager to begin his work. Meeting with Moston was only a formality. He'd already done deep research on both employer and target. Moston was a sad little man who'd lost the only interesting thing about himself when his wife disappeared. He had few friends, his family dead or estranged. He did not work, instead living on his wife's money. His sole hobby appeared to be mourning. Their meeting had not caused Gabrogian to suspect the man's motives were anything other than what they appeared to be. Moston's life was an open book, albeit a trite and quotidian tale.

Volscher, on the other hand, was a different story. Gabrogian's research yielded precious little on the enigmatic protector of decaying places. He'd conducted numerous interviews since arriving in Benoit. Street people. Hustlers of all stripes. A few police officers he'd had business with before, who could be counted on for their discretion. All told the same tale, as though they spoke with a single voice—the sigil, the dictates, the penalties.

He'd also unearthed several decades-old newspaper articles, written by one Elza Lenolka, concerning a series of unconnected-yet-mysterious disappearances. Every victim vanished randomly, usually at night but sometimes during the day. They ranged from drifters to the professional classes, doctors and lawyers. Lenolka could uncover no intersections between their lives, such as a soup kitchen the impoverished frequented where the professionals also volunteered. These were all people who did not and could not know one another, most lacking enemies or motivations to disappear themselves such as affairs or bad debts. But every one, gone without a trace. Volscher was not mentioned by name, but several of the victims had last been seen near abandoned buildings or other lonely sites.

Lenolka herself had vanished, mere weeks after publishing her last article. Her fiancé—now covered in liver spots, gnarled hands pushing pawns across a chessboard in the park—confirmed she'd gone to investigate an abandoned pump house near the Steelhead, allegedly with another reporter, but that reporter denied any knowledge of the supposed meeting. The fiancé suspected this final lie was one in a long string of them, so he wouldn't worry about her as she visited the dark and seedy spaces of the city on her own.

The places that finally, apparently, took her.

The signs of what was happening in Benoit were apparent to Gabrogian. Some dark and prehistoric shape swam here in the depths, unseen except for the ripples it caused when snatching another victim. Gabrogian had met many such things.

And ended them.

He neared the end of Elscolm Avenue. The broken trestle lay just ahead, gleaming like flayed bones in the moonlight.

IV.

Moston sat in a chair at his bedroom window, sipping whisky from a tumbler and staring out into the night. Pavrachak's *Symphony No. 2* played on the phonograph at his bedside, as it had every night since Annelina's disappearance. She herself held no particular love for the composer, but for Moston, it recalled the early days in their relationship when they would walk arm-in-arm down the cobblestone streets of the Seventh Fortissiment, the strains of dozens of violins seeping out of half-open tenement windows.

For Annelina, their dates doubled as scouting expeditions. Her firm ended up buying up the tenement houses and tearing them down to build a shopping center. In retrospect, he wasn't surprised his wife's vocation put her on a collision course with Volscher. After all, she had dedicated her life to urban renewal—the literal definition of cross purposes. Moston wished Annelina had been an accountant or lawyer. Or anything, really, other than a re-inventor of withered and crumbling spaces. But then she would not have been who she was, and though he might still have loved her, it would not have been the same kind of love.

And then, if she'd died anyway, neither would it have been the same kind of mourning.

The glass of whisky was cold in his hand. He finished the last of it and went to pour himself another.

The wet bar was on the first floor. He padded down the stairs, gripped with the now-familiar feeling he was walking through an unfamiliar place, some oneirological re-assemblage of the rooms he'd shared with Annelina. He had not removed any of her things or even rearranged them, but much of the furniture had been draped in white sheets, as he had little use for it now. Everything looked different.

The smell of the place had changed as well. The floral scents he'd always associated with Annelina—from favored perfumes and the bouquets he regularly purchased her—were gone. Now the stench of mildew filled all three floors of the house. Moston could not locate its source, no matter how diligently he searched. He sometimes heard a phantom drip in the attic when it rained, but his explorations of the narrow, insulated space were fruitless.

Slowly, every single day, the stench got a little worse.

After replenishing his drink, Moston resumed his vigil by the window. From his vantage point, he could not actually see the abandoned train trestle over the Steelhead River, or indeed any point nearby. Other places of Volscher's were far closer, including a burned-out rowhouse on the next block. The eyesore dragged down property values, but no one dared reclaim it—not even Annelina, who abandoned her overtures to the property's absentee owner for reasons she never revealed.

Moston had flirted with using the rowhouse, so he could surreptitiously observe what he'd set in motion, but in the end, it seemed poetic to send Gabrogian to the place Annelina disappeared. The fact it lay miles away from Moston's own home was entirely coincidental.

Since all he could do was wait for word from Gabrogian, Moston stared out his window at the shadowed skyline of his city, indulging the worst kinds of magical thinking. Vigilantly attuned to any imperceptible change in the character of the buildings or the play of the moonlight indicating Gabrogian had succeeded, and Volscher was dead.

Or that the mercenary had failed, and the shape of the city would hold, static, until the very foundations of the buildings crumbled and the towers collapsed into dust.

Completing Volscher's claim to Benoit in toto.

PRESERVATION

V.

It was windy there, on that broken trestle over the Steelhead River. Gusts burned Gabrogian's cheeks and buffeted the remains of his wiry black hair. He did not wrap his coat around himself, but let it hang open so he could access his tool. The cold was noted but did not bother him in any meaningful way.

The work kept him warm.

Off to his right, traffic flowed over the new bridge. An errant horn occasionally echoed across the river. Otherwise, the night was silent save for the lap of water against the trestle's struts.

The trestle itself was not long, only extending ten feet over the water before breaking off, the remains of the track either submerged beneath the river's surface or hauled away by city workers sometime before the claiming of this place by the Volscher entity.

Gabrogian walked the trestle carefully. Every step was treacherous thanks to well-rotted wood and rust-speckled iron that looked ready to break apart. A poor place for a fight. Or at least a conventional one, though Gabrogian was well-suited for any sort of battle. He didn't know what Volscher was, not exactly, but suspected him kin to the other anomalies he'd encountered, and wiped from the world with little more than a slash of his blade and a firm conviction things like them should not be. Or at least as closely related as things of their nature could be, their primary defining characteristics being malevolence and otherness.

The wind brought with it a salty scent, carried from the place where the Steelhead flowed into the sea. Ashore, the city lights twinkled pleasantly. He'd fought in worse places to die.

Near the end of the trestle, he found some markings in the rotting wood. Dropping to his haunches, he inspected the marks. Just what Moston said he'd find—a bisected figure eight.

Gabrogian removed a serrated combat knife from the leather sheath at his belt. The handle was wrapped in electrical tape, the blade scratched and pitted, though well-sharp. There was little remarkable about it, but an ordinary knife in his hand was as good as a blessed silver dagger in any other's, because he had learned one thing throughout his voluminous transactions over the years. It was not the weapon, it was the will—the calm, cold surety, war-born and long-crystallized in the cavity a normal man's heart might occupy, that he possessed the capacity to triumph against any odds. *That* was what he killed with, and he'd yet to find a creature immune to it.

He murmured a prayer to himself, the only god he believed in. Then he slashed at Volscher's symbol until it splintered into oblivion.

Gabrogian rose, eyes and ears keen, knife at the ready. His heart thumped along at forty beats per minute.

This was the moment he loved best—the conflict assured, the outcome decided in his mind, his only task to make such a vision manifest. In these moments he thought himself an artist, or perhaps a mother, bringing forth something into the world that had never before existed—the non-existence of his quarry.

After all, destruction is just another form of creation.

PRESERVATION

Based on what Moston told him—not that Gabrogian trusted his employer entirely, or at all—the Volscher entity should appear immediately, perhaps materializing out of the darkness around the trestle or rising from the depths of the Steelhead. Depending on the creature's nature, an attack could come from above, below, or even within the depths of his own mind.

But no such attack came. Gabrogian continued to scan the trestle, the night around him, the sky above. Nothing. Nor did his senses, finely attuned to things that interrupted the natural order, indicate anything was amiss. The air smelled like the river, and little else.

Perhaps Moston had been mistaken about the Volscher entity's nature, or its existence. A hazard in Gabrogian's line of work—on occasion, he found his time wasted on urban legends built on the slightest scaffolding of truth. His clients were well-meaning, or in some cases deluded, but the result was the same.

Gabrogian left town disappointed, his knife clean as when he'd arrived.

A soft *plop* came from the water below. He glanced down—nothing but ripples. No pale creature emerged to pull him beneath the surface, no hungry maw parted the waters to consume him. His coat did feel off, though. He patted his breast pocket—his cell phone was gone?

And then he realized he could no longer feel the wind.

It was still blowing. That much was obvious, the trees were swaying on the shore. A plastic bag at the end of the trestle danced in a draft.

Curious.

Gabrogian licked the tip of his index finger and held it to the sky. Nothing.

He tensed, raised his knife, heartbeat rising to fifty beats a second in his excitement.

The moment.

Again he scanned his surroundings. The night was still and silent. And yet, the water—

The water was a shade lighter than it had been when he'd first walked the trestle. Barely a degree's difference, but unmistakable to Gabrogian's keen eyes and infallible memory. He glanced at the moon to see if perhaps a cloud had drifted in front of it, altering the light.

The sky was cloudless, but the moon itself was also—no better, more precise term for it—wrong. Transparent, insubstantial, hanging in the sky like a piece of gauze. Gabrogian thought he could reach out and rip it in two.

The water, the sky, even the trestle itself looked bleached. Washed out. Still, he felt no wind, yet he saw signs of it touching his surroundings. And the night, already quiet, was quieter still—traffic passed at a slow clip over the new bridge, but now it did so in complete silence.

Volscher.

Gabrogian fell to his haunches again and poked at the sigil with the tip of his blade. It passed through the disfigured figure eight, like through a hologram. And yet it had been real enough when he'd brought his blade to bear moments earlier.

His pulse quickened. This was new. Was he imagining this? Or had he imagined everything up until this moment? Had he dreamed a dream of Argo Gabrogian, trotting from city to city to slaughter the

PRESERVATION

things that impinged on the order of the world? All this time, had he simply been a ghost haunting a broken trestle over the Steelhead River, who didn't want to believe he was dead?

No. Gabrogian calmed his thoughts. Volscher was doing this. Some sort of foul trick.

Gabrogian might not be able to touch the world around him, but he would find a way to touch that devil.

"Volscher!" he screamed into the night. "Face me! Face me, you coward!"

The night replied with silence. Nothing appeared. The moon faded further, then the river and the trestle. Even the sound of water slapping against the struts was hardly more than a small tinny echo—perhaps his sole tenuous connection to the rapidly-receding world around him.

He kicked the trestle. Or tried, his foot passed through the rusted iron like smoke. His brow furrowed—how was he still standing? Why hadn't he fallen into the river, or *beyond* it, hurtling through layers of silt and rock into the burning molten heart of the Earth itself? But no, he seemed to be suspended in approximately the same place he'd been standing.

Gabrogian hurried down the trestle, towards shore. There, perhaps the world would come back into focus, and then he could find a way to fight. But before he reached the bank, his surroundings completed their long fade into nothingness, and now there was nothing to walk on, nowhere to walk *to*. Above, below, on either side—concepts which had lost all meaning—there was nothing.

After a time, Gabrogian sat down heavily—upon nothing—and waited.

For what, he did not know.

VI.

Well past one in the morning, Moston was on his fourth glass of whisky. His head swam, his eyelids grew heavy. Booze did not become him. He'd never been a committed drinker, although he'd tried his best in the months since Annelina's disappearance.

Still, he kept his vigil by the window, alert to any change in the city's character, however slight. He checked his cell phone incessantly, paranoid he'd missed a call from Gabrogian, though as the night dragged on he thought it less likely he'd ever hear from the man.

Moston sighed and slumped in his chair. His plans for revenge were misguided at best. Whatever Volscher was, he was beyond Moston's reach. If Annelina had been killed by an errant lightning strike, would he have tried to assassinate the sky? He should've just accepted that his life had been taken from him with no hope of remedy or recourse.

Pavrachak played on, on and on. The endless musical loop offered a bleak preview of the days ahead. Sleep, wake, remember. Drink. Few things interested him. Film and television held no appeal. Foods tasted bland now, no matter the artistry employed in their preparation. Pavrachak he only played to remember, he derived no joy from the music.

And travel? Where would he go? All places were the same, fundamentally. Any place he went would have streets, people, trees. Maybe even bizarre godlings lurking in sad and broken places, waiting for someone to come along and violate their arbitrary rules.

PRESERVATION

No. He would stay here, and let the house fall down around him.

He slept—badly, like he did all things—and awoke some time later. The glass of whisky had tumbled from his hand, spilling melted ice across the hardwood floor. On the bedside table, the phonograph droned on.

But the room was colder than it had been.

Moston leaned forward to look out the window, to search for any signs of dawn on the horizon. As he exhaled, his breath clung to the glass and slowly resolved into a familiar shape. He leaned back, rubbing his eyes, hoping it was some trick of his sleep-befogged mind.

It was not. Volscher's sigil, born of Moston's breath, stained the windowpane. The rowhouse was now his.

Moston laughed. At first a tiny eruption—almost a hiccup—it soon grew into a thunderous, mirthless guffaw that shook his entire body and brought tears to his eyes. He fell to the floor, pounding the hardwood with his fists. He smashed his whisky glass, slicing open his hand. Blood spurted from the wound and dripped onto the wood. The window, the chair, the melting ice cubes on the floor all faded around him.

And soon enough, the laughter became a scream.

VII.

Argo Gabrogian was surrounded by nothing.

He had no sense of how long he'd been there, in such a nowhere. *Ridiculous*. How could he be nowhere? Maybe he wasn't, maybe he simply lacked a place in which to be. The distinction was purely academic.

He'd miscalculated, underestimated this Volscher. Proceeded under the foolish assumption it was similar to the things he'd encountered before—all alike, give or take some teeth, appendages, or degrees of corporeality. But no. This thing was different, possessed of a nature and a power unfathomable.

Somehow, it had excised him completely from the rest of existence.

Gabrogian had never doubted himself, not on the battlefields that marked the first half of his life nor in the dark alleys that delineated the second. But now, stripped of all agency, his only option was to wait—perhaps for nothing. For however long, he could not know, for he'd been cleanly sheared from time as well as space.

Alone, impossibly alone, he sat and brooded and wondered how long it might be before he turned his knife, and more importantly his will, upon himself.

THE SIREN SONG OF SHARP AND DEADLY THINGS

ON THOSE RARE evenings when fate conspired to make John close all by his lonesome, Giuseppe's seemed stuffed to bursting with untold perils.

Most nights, when the restaurant filled with Mission Beach refugees trailing sand across the floor from their unraveling towels, Giuseppe's appeared bright and cheery, if a little dated, and everything a pizza parlor should be—red-and-white checked tablecloths, air redolent with baking dough and oozily melting cheese, families huddled at tables leveled out with red pepper packets, chewing greasy slices and telling each other through mouthfuls of dough how very *fun* it all was. Even the local burnouts who came for the two-dollar beers and stayed for the Ms. Pacman machine were a source of comfort for John, though their swearing tended to intimidate the more uptight patrons.

Because John knew with all these people around, he wouldn't be tempted to do anything *crazy*.

His boss George, a tattooed ex-Texan with a mohawk and the sort of obsequious manner that made tourists picture him as a clean-cut Mormon missionary in their rose-tinted vacation memories, usually cut John early, though he didn't mind working late.

He just hated to be alone in the restaurant.

Not that it was haunted or anything. John was a staunch (and, if you asked his friends, annoying) atheist. Completely unlike George, who'd filmed a series of amateur ghost-hunting videos where he ran around in the dark and screamed at every mote of dust that caught his flashlight until his girlfriend insisted he devote his free time to pursuing a vague associate degree.

No, when John was alone in the pizza parlor in the shadow of the Belmont Park roller coaster, he didn't peer into dark corners, starting at spectral faces, or jump at every creak and moan as the old building settled.

Nor did he worry about getting robbed—Giuseppe's was a pizza place, not a diamond exchange.

What frightened John so much about an empty Giuseppe's was the simple fact that it hadn't been *John-proofed.*

A casual visitor to John's studio apartment a dozen blocks north might not notice anything amiss. They'd only see the kind of cramped apartment common to twenty-somethings living beachside. A single futon in the middle of the stained greenish carpet, crumpled comforter curled up on it like a sleeping dog. A TV, Xbox with various games scattered in front. A kitchenette off to the right, food-encrusted dishes in

THE SIREN SONG OF SHARP & DEADLY THINGS

the sink, a sauce-spattered microwave next to a narrow refrigerator. On the other side of the apartment, a tiny bathroom with alley view.

Nothing too unusual, right? Just a rusty beach cruiser and wobbly skateboard elucidating his hobbies. A stack of DVDs, X-rated spines turned towards the wall in the unlikely event of a female visitor. A couple books on the floor by the futon: vintage Barker, Richard Thomas, *The Big Book of Haunted GPS Stories*.

But hold on.

This whole place is a mask.

John's not a normal guy, and I'll show you why. Look in the silverware drawer.

Notice anything?

Exactly—no actual silverware. Plastic sporks a-plenty, and that's it. No knives, forks, or spoons.

Maybe he's just broke? But wait, there's more.

Check out the stove.

No, not the congealed grease around the burners. Look around back, and try not to think about what might be growing on the wall.

The stove's not hooked up, is it?

Let's check out the cabinet below the sink. A fresh pack of sponges, some dish soap. No Drano, no bleach. No real cleaning products of any kind, but you could have guessed that from the crap caked on the counters, right?

Hmm.

On with the tour. There's a wardrobe tucked away in a corner, or as tucked away as anything can be in a single room with off-white walls and a popcorn ceiling. Inside, you've got your shirts, pants, a drawer filled with unpaired socks and underwear. No belts.

Wait, maybe there's one looped through those pants under the futon?

Nope.

Time to check the bathroom.

So small, just a closet you can shit in, though I suppose you could shit in any closet with the proper motivation. What's stopping you?

Something's growing in the sink. There's a toothbrush and squeezed-out tube of paste by the grimy faucet handles. An electric razor, one of those Star Trek phaser-looking things, blinks *ready* from its charging stand.

It's not polite, but while we're here let's snoop around in the medicine cabinet.

Practically nothing. No drugs, not even a bottle of Tylenol. Nail clippers—the sharpest thing in the entire house. *Lectric Shave.* Deodorant, a necessity for those long and sweaty shifts worked in close proximity to a pizza oven.

That's it.

The toilet's new, a low-flow model. A strange sight in a crumbling budget beach rental. The tub's just a tub, mildew patterns making it a snowflake in its own way. No stopper in sight.

Most guys John's age probably don't take baths. So maybe it's not that odd.

In fact, nothing in the apartment is, taken by itself. Just run-of-the-mill bachelor shit. But added together?

Think about it.

First-floor apartment. No knives in the kitchen, no chemicals under the sink. No way to turn on the gas stove. No belts or razor blades or pills to pour down your greedy gullet. Not even a stopper to fill the tub the requisite two inches needed to drown a person.

Yeah, think about it.

Here's a list of things John can do in his apartment:

Watch TV, play video games, read, microwave noodles, shower, shave poorly, sing a song, brush his teeth. Jack off.

Here's a list of things John *can't* do in his apartment:

Kill himself.

The only time John tripped on acid he'd been pinballing around some dark basement party, nodding to the same twelve people over and over again when the cops broke it up. After he'd wandered the streets until he ran into a girl he knew from sociology—drunk and spilling tears because she couldn't find her friends—and they'd gone back to her sixth-story apartment where she promptly passed out. John tried to watch TV but none of the shows made sense. Picked up a magazine and flipped through, the pages like colored-in placemats at Denny's, just random spidery lines crawling all over the glossy paper. So he'd gone out to her balcony to smoke.

John leaned up against the railing despite the light drizzle and lit up.

Then he made the mistake of looking *down*.

The parking lot was lit up like a nativity scene, illuminating a handful of cars parked in neat rows. Droplets of rain glittered like diamonds on the asphalt. Beautiful. And the more John looked the *closer* it all seemed to be. Like he could reach out and touch it. All that stood between him and the parking lot was this flimsy filigreed railing. He could toss one leg over, then the other, and he'd be *there*.

So. Close.

So pretty.

To be down there, among the raindrops, seemed the most important thing in the world.

John had one leg over the railing when his cigarette burned all the way down.

The cherry scorched his skin. He cried out, dropping the butt, watching it tumble end over end to the wet asphalt, where it sizzled briefly and then lay still.

He pictured himself, falling like the butt.

Landing on the wet asphalt.

Lying *still*.

He clenched that railing, hands shaking, his breath coming fast now, heart pounding. The spasming in his hands moved up his forearms, jittering his elbows, shaking his shoulders. John hung on for dear life.

He didn't want to fall like that cigarette, to see the ground rising up to meet him faster and faster like that old Irish prayer, before the impact burst him like a fleshy, blood-filled balloon.

May the road rise up to meet you.

No, John thought, *may it not. I don't want that, I don't—*

Oh yeah.

He carefully pulled his leg over the railing and staggered back into the shut sliding glass door. Then he took a deep breath and went back inside.

THE SIREN SONG OF SHARP & DEADLY THINGS

His host found him in the morning, huddled behind the couch, shaking and mumbling to himself.

But alive.

And *aware*.

That was the last fucking time John ever touched LSD.

John thought about suicide. A lot.

Not about doing it himself. He liked his life. Stuff went wrong, girls broke up with him, he came up short on rent. But nothing ever went *that* wrong, and he rarely got depressed.

No, John thought about suicide *in general*. Why people did it, sure. But more about how easy it was. Drink that drain cleaner under the sink. Grab that knife and cut *down,* not across, this ain't a cry for help. Wrap that belt around your neck.

Just do it.

John would lie on his futon, the covers pulled up to his nose, looking around his apartment, thinking about all the things he could use to off himself.

If he wanted to.

Which he didn't.

But damn would it be easy if he did.

Maybe not easy, really. What's so easy about drinking bleach and feeling your spine reassert itself into a question mark while your insides burn? Not *easy*.

But possible.

And that was somehow worse.

John lived in constant terror he might be gripped by some sort of temporary insanity and off himself before he even knew what he was doing. He just couldn't trust himself, not after that rainy night out on the balcony.

A fraction of a second. That's all it would take.

And he'd be dead.

No more *Madden,* no more scarfing pizza and slamming beers and listening to Lagwagon while skating the boardwalk, eyes behind shades, 007-ing every tanned and top-heavy girl who jogged past. Everything, gone in an instant.

So John cleaned house. Ditched the drain cleaner, the steak knives, even his hard alcohol, since he'd heard a story about some dead frat boy who'd butt-chugged a bottle of vodka.

No drugs, no chemicals, no sharp objects, that's how John lived. And he did.

Live, that is.

Just another night at Giuseppe's.

A couple of Irish guys from the hostel walked in with their dates and took a table in the corner. Local chicks, taken by their accents and lopsided grins, how they swore casually and drank professionally, both young men milking their national origin for all it was worth. John took their drink order. As he turned to fill it, a couple of the local burnouts oozed in and John had to remind them to leave their skateboards by the door. They scurried off to their usual spot by the Ms. Pacman machine. John dropped off a pitcher of Bud Light automatically to keep the natives from getting restless.

The night passed in a flurry of Hawaiian slices and

Caesar salads. Granules of parmesan rained like snow. John ran beers and food, checks and change. Pushed drinks out of the way to drop steaming hot pies in the middle of the table, slicing them with the freshly-sharpened pizza cutter he kept in his apron. John had the floor to himself, while George slaved away in front of the implacably hungry oven since the usual cook called in. Most of the night, everything went fine.

Until George started screaming.

"Dude, you okay?" John yelled, slipping and sliding on the black-and-white checked floor, nearly taking a header into the soda machine.

George stood in front of the oven, face flushed, a supreme pizza flipped upside down at his feet, holding a wet towel over his hand. "Fuckin' burned myself. *Bad.*"

Then he unwrapped the towel.

The ridge of knuckles along George's right hand was horribly charred, so cracked and burnt, something white winking at John beneath the wreck.

John staggered back, smacking his spine against the wall, and for a moment he was back on that balcony, straddling the railing that wanted him over it so fucking bad. He shook his head and said, "You want me to call 911?"

"Nah, you know Paola doesn't give us health insurance. Call Ronnie. She's got a couple girlfriends. Nurses. Phone's in my bag." He gestured at his backpack with his chin, tendons straining.

"I got you," John said, unzipping the outer pocket of the backpack and pulling out George's phone.

"Code's nine five seven three," George said through gritted teeth. "This shit *hurts.*"

"Nine five seven three," John echoed. "Just hold on." He dialed Ronnie, put the phone to his ear. It seemed to ring on forever, while George groaned and pulled the towel off his hand, wetting it in the sink before re-wrapping it.

"Fucked up my tattoo."

"What?" John asked between rings.

In response, George held up his left fist. *Free* tattooed across his knuckles.

The right said *Live,* which John always found confusing because his boss was from Texas, not New Hampshire.

But after a burn like that, no way George's right hand said a goddamn thing.

Live was gone. *Free* was all that was left.

Fat crackled and popped in the oven. John turned to look at the dancing flames. Thought about how a man of his size might be able to fit the upper half of his body in, no problem. Just enough to cook the flesh right off his head and shoulders.

He almost dropped the phone, then realized someone on the other end was saying, "Hello? Hello," over and over.

"Hey, it's John. From the restaurant?" George groaned in the background. "George had an accident. I mean, he's *okay,* it's just his hand—"

"Jesus, I keep telling him he needs to get the hell out of there. Okay, hold tight, I'm on my way."

"Thanks," John replied, but she'd already hung up. "She's coming," he said to George.

George nodded, skin bleached white like the sacks of flour in the back. "I'll go wait outside. So I don't bother the—" his face twisted in agony, "*customers.*"

"Need anything?"

THE SIREN SONG OF SHARP & DEADLY THINGS

George grunted and turned for the back door. "Just come check on me in a minute. Make sure I'm not passed out."

"Will do."

"Hey," an exaggerated Irish brogue called from the seating area. "We'd fancy another drink."

John hurried over to the taps. The back door swung shut.

"Hey bro," one of the burnouts said through the unruly mop of salt-encrusted hair hanging in his eyes, holding out an empty pitcher. "Hook it up."

"Got it!" John attacked the taps. Sweat streamed down his forehead. Usually, work jazzed him. Now, with George's injury, he just felt sick, and they weren't even busy. He hoped he wouldn't hear the jingle-jangle of the front door.

Of course he did.

John choked off the taps and spun around. A young couple wearing UCSD sweatshirts stood in the doorway, peering at him through identical glasses. "Sit anywhere you like," John said quickly, then snatched up the round earmarked for the Irish delegation. Turning, he nearly bumped into one of the burnouts.

"You mind if I just grab that?" the guy asked, gesturing a leathery paw at the pitcher sitting beneath the row of taps.

Only employees were allowed behind the bar, but considering the only *other* employee had been attacked by an angry pizza oven, John figured why the hell not. "Go for it."

He plopped the drinks down on the Irish table and hurried over to the students, who were uneasily adjusting themselves in their chairs and took their order. As he hurried back to the soda fountain he sniffed the air. Underneath the sickly sweet smell of George's scorched flesh, something was burning.

"Oh, fuck," John muttered and rushed back to the oven.

Black smoke spewed from the machine. John squinted through the fumes and flames, spotted the dark circular outline of a charring pie somewhere in the back.

"Excuse me," a woman snapped. "We're ready to *order*."

John whipped his head around. One of the college students stood *behind* the counter, arms crossed.

"We've got a little problem," John said dumbly, gesturing at the smoking pizza oven.

The woman shook her head in disgust. "I *knew* we should have gone to Olive Garden."

John felt like an idiot for seating her in the first place. Even if his oven hadn't gone loco, he didn't know how to make a pizza unless it came wrapped in plastic.

Which made him picture what he might want on his own tombstone.

The oven belched more smoke. John gaped at the mounting disaster, his mind completely blank.

And then he had an idea.

Not a useful one, nothing to do with putting the fire *out*. No, for some reason, putting his hand *in* that roaring metallic mouth seemed like the finest thing in the world. He'd seen what it did to George, and that was before the flames had turned full-on apocalyptic. If he stuck his hand in there now, the oven would probably scorch him down to the bone in seconds.

The acrid stench of smoke turned into the sweet,

drizzling pork-fat stink of his own charbroiling skin. Saliva flooded his mouth as his hand reached for the oven.

John shuddered and wrenched himself away, grabbing the fire extinguisher off the wall. He read the instructions while the fire burned ever hotter, wiping sweat out of his eyes.

Maybe I should call 911. But then he pictured firefighters stomping into the restaurant, taking one look at the burning oven, then shaking their heads in disgust and stomping back out.

"Fuck it," he said, pulling the pin and spraying the oven. A white cloud of carbon dioxide battled the black cloud of burning pizza for a brief moment, then overtook it. The flames sputtered and died. John surveyed his handiwork, breathing heavily, the empty extinguisher hanging at his side. He'd done it. Put the fire out, *and* shut up the stupid voice in the back of his head. John nodded once, then walked out back to check on George.

George was sitting against the cement wall, next to the dumpster, smoking a cigarette.

"Need anything?" John asked.

"Feeling better already. Maybe I just needed a smoke. Ha!" The words tumbled out a little too quickly, a little too loud.

"All right. Look, the oven caught on fire so I had to spray it with the fire extinguisher."

George took a drag of his cigarette, exhaling up into the night. "That piece of shit. Did the same thing to me, before you started. Man, it's—" George squeezed his eyes shut. After a moment his face relaxed again, and he continued, "—it's a bitch to clean."

A pair of headlights turned down the alley. *Ronnie.* "So, I don't see any reason to stay open—"

"Yeah, no shit. Close everybody out and put a sign on the door. The beach creatures'll throw a fit, but tell them the Pennant's got two dollar you-call-its tonight."

"It does?"

"No, but by the time they get there they won't give a shit. Maybe give 'em one for the road in a to-go cup."

"Yeah."

The headlights got closer—Ronnie's Accord.

"My ride's here," George said, stubbing out his cigarette and hauling himself to his feet.

"Take care of yourself, man."

George looked at his wounded hand. "You too. This place'll get you if you're not careful."

John turned to go back inside and realized he'd forgotten to prop the back door open. He'd have to go around front. He waved to Ronnie, helping George with his seat belt, and hurried down the alley. Out front, he scoped the scene. The college students looked pissed. The burnouts were half-playing Ms. Pacman and half-looking for their next pitcher. The Irish contingent laughed animatedly, smacking their table. John surveyed the situation and figured out who he'd get rid of first. College kids, one. Burnouts, two. Hibernians and dates, three. He took a deep breath and stepped inside. Wanting eyes turned to watch his progress. Nobody ever looked at him without wanting something.

Not even the silverware.

He stopped by the cash register for a gift card, then took it over to the college kids with a song and dance about technical difficulties. Their expressions

THE SIREN SONG OF SHARP & DEADLY THINGS

softened at the prospect of free shit, and they left happy, maybe bound for Olive Garden.

Next, he filled some to-go cups with Bud Light to offer the burnouts. The prospect of going somewhere else clearly troubled them, as they were as much a part of Giuseppe's as the dented tin sign over the bar calling out all thirty-two NFL teams. But when John pressed free beer into their leathery hands and lied about the specials at the Pennant, they acquiesced, leaving behind an unfinished game of Ms. Pacman. The avatar waited silently in the center of the maze for the ghosts to consume her.

That just left the Irish. John printed their check and took it to the table. As he approached, the Irish guys raised their glasses to cheers, coaxing their dates into doing the same. He didn't hear what they said.

He heard something else entirely.

May the road rise up to meet you.

And all of a sudden he was *back,* tripping balls on a balcony, balancing over the railing, center of gravity drifting, the raindrops sparkled on the pavement and he was plummeting, the parking lot rising up to meet him, getting closer and closer and—

"Hey mate, I said which way's the jacks?"

John gaped at the shorter of the Irishmen, his mouth dry. "The jacks?"

"The *bathroom.*"

The guy was laying it on so thick John could barely understand him. He pointed towards the back.

"Thanks," the guy said, getting up. "Give us another round, will you?"

John held the check out. "We're closing early. There's a problem with the kitchen—"

"There a problem with the bloody taps?"

"No—"

"Then what's the harm in getting us one more?"

"Sorry, my manager told me to close up."

"All right, then. Donal, pay the man."

"Ah, it's your bloody turn, you—"

The voices faded out, and John just willed them to shut up and get on with it until the check was pushed back into his hands.

"Keep the change."

John nodded and walked into the back. He looked around for something to write on, finally tearing the top off a pizza box and inking *Closed Early—Come See Us Again*. When he walked back into the front to tape the sign to the door, the restaurant was empty. Through the roller coaster decal on the window, the Irish guys threw arms around their dates and shepherded them away to greener pastures.

Thank god.

His customers were nice enough, but John was desperate to head home—the adrenaline spike of dealing with the oven fire was fading, leaving him exhausted, physically and mentally, and more than a little disturbed at the lingering memory of George's wound.

John started picking up. As he bussed tables people looked in from outside, pressing their faces against the glass, at least until they noticed the closed sign on the door. The whole restaurant felt like a fishbowl. John shivered and kept working.

As he walked back to drop the dirty dishes at the dish pit, he noticed the gleaming rack of kitchen knives. The way the fluorescent lights lent a pinprick shine to their tips. And he couldn't help but wonder what it might be like to have that shine inside of him.

THE SIREN SONG OF SHARP & DEADLY THINGS

To take the sharpest knife off the rack and dig it into his forearm, welcoming it into yielding flesh. He could do it—the knives were *right there.*

It would be easy.

Or at least possible.

The weight of the plates in John's hands brought him back to earth with a shudder. He'd almost done it again, gotten lost in thought and gotten way too close to—he didn't even want to *think* it.

He took the dishes back to the pit. Looked at the spray nozzle hanging there like a malignant vine. Wondered how hot the water could get. He could fill the sink with boiling water, plunge his face in like he was bobbing for apples, and the flesh would bubble right off and when he opened his mouth to scream the water would rush down his throat, scouring his insides.

"Goddammit," John muttered, putting the dishes down. He had to get out of there. George, his coworkers, probably even Paola herself, none of them saw Giuseppe's the way *he* did. Any of them, in his position, would be trudging up and down the rows of tables cleaning up, maybe snatching fistfuls of croutons from the salad bar to power them through the next half hour. All they'd think about was what they'd be doing when they left. What they'd eat or what they'd drink or who they'd fuck.

The pizza oven grinned at him. John shot it the finger and hurried out front. Talking heads on mute chattered away on the TVs, power cords hanging like cobwebs beneath them. He wondered about that current. If he started chewing his way through the cords like a rat, would that be enough?

No, he assured himself. He might get a little jolt, but no way a TV cord could kill him.

If so, he'd have to lose *his* TV, and there went half his hobbies.

Screw this.

John opened the cash register. He could just put the night's take in the safe, then cut out. Everything else could wait. He'd leave a note for the morning shift. Tell them he was coming back first thing to help them clean up.

Lights danced on the jukebox, threatening to come to life without the benefit of a smoothed-out dollar and blast David Lee Roth's lectures about what he *might as well do.*

Come on, John. Why don't you go ahead and—

He was counting out cash on the bartop when a glint caught his eye.

A forgotten fork, lying tines-up beneath one of the tables.

Pictured himself running over, snatching up the fork, plunging it directly into his eye. Sticking it through the gelatinous mass as far as it could go, and when it stuck, when he ran low on will or strength?

Grabbing both sides of the table, rearing back his head, blood and eyeball fluid pinkly sluicing down his cheek, the end of the fork sticking up in the air like someone's finger when they're trying to make a point, *excuse me sir,* the fan above chop-chop-chopping the air, egging him on, and then banging his head forward, plunging down down *down* towards the table—

John screamed and ran for the door, leaving the money where it was. He hauled ass down the street, arms and legs pumping wildly. He'd left the door unlocked, but it didn't matter. If he spent one more second in that place . . .

THE SIREN SONG OF SHARP & DEADLY THINGS

He staggered to a halt next to a bus bench, heaving ragged breaths, watching a pair of headlights barreling down the street. Probably a drunk, driving way too fast for the twenty-five-mile speed limit on Mission Boulevard. He was already standing on the curb, headlights rushing closer and all he had to do was step off—

The car zoomed past and John opened his eyes, realized he'd wrapped himself around the street sign like a koala, clinging on for dear life.

He stuck to the alleys the rest of the way home. Sketchy, drug-addled bundles of rags eyed John when he passed, but he ignored them. They didn't scare him.

At home, it took his trembling hands three tries to get the key in the lock, but then the door mercifully swung open. His apartment was dark and welcoming, like a return to the womb. John stepped inside, closing and locking the door behind him, shaking with relief. He tried not to think about work, about what he'd done. The morning shift would be pissed at how he'd left it, and that was provided no one took advantage of the door he'd forgotten to lock and swiped everything from the money on the counter to the cleaning supplies in the hall closet.

A sob welled up inside him. John leaned against the doorframe and slowly sunk to the floor. Why was he like *this?* Why couldn't he just be *normal?*

When his butt hit the floor, something clinked in the apron he'd forgotten to take off. Dumbly, he reached into the pocket and wrapped his fingers around a plastic handle. He slowly pulled the object out.

His pizza cutter, the metal edge crusted red with dry marinara sauce.

Without thinking, he flicked it. The metal disc spun round and round. Faster and faster and faster yet. Mesmerizing.

His finger was bleeding—sharp. The pizza cutter was *that* sharp.

And now he was all alone with it.

John didn't want to kill himself. He didn't want to jump off a balcony or chug drain cleaner or press a shotgun barrel to the fat under his chin.

But all alone in his apartment with the pizza cutter, so keen-edged, so enthralling, so tantalizing—

How could he *not?*

GHOSTS OF FREDERICKSBURG

SURE, I'VE GOT a ghost story.

Seems like most people do, and why shouldn't we? We're the kind of creatures who look up at the night sky and draw patterns in the stars, squinting at far-off balls of plasma until they look like crabs or bulls or a guy with a bow. We've got brains that are maybe too big for hunting and gathering and too small for navigating the complexities of a world that's risen seemingly unbidden around us. Compounding information and instincts collide in those singular organs until our imaginations run away from us like horses over the hills. One part pattern-seeking, two parts fight-or-flight, three parts a desire to separate from the pack, to feel like we've gained some special insight denied the rest of the clan.

We can all conjure spirits. At one point or another, most of us do.

Yeah, I've got a ghost story.

Let's call her Anya.

I met her at the restaurant where we both worked, a fine dining establishment attached to one of the two gay bars in a small southern town on the verge of getting sucked up into the vast suburban sprawl of the greater Washington, D.C. metropolitan area. Wilcox's, it was called—the previous owner's surname. The current owner had certainly put his stamp on the place, with the faux-marble wallpaper that called to mind a Grecian bath. And the fist-sized holes in the drywall, the odd shard of shattered ashtray we'd find in the carpets, and the omnipresent surveillance cameras that gave him a bird's-eye view of every square inch of the property from the second-floor aerie that served as both apartment and office.

Wilcox's was situated on Caroline Street, downtown Fredericksburg's main drag, in a historic row house sandwiched between a tobacconist and a B&B. Caroline Street seemed a bit unsure of itself—a mishmash of upscale restaurants and dive bars, tattoo parlors, and curio shops hocking *Virginia is for Lovers* schwag, check-cashing counters, and stores stocked with toys only children centuries-dead would want to play with like nutcrackers and rocking horses. A street trying to be all things to all people, from the civil servants who took the DC-bound train every day to the students at the local university, from the tour buses of old folks in search of authenticity and useless knick-knacks to the out-and-proud rednecks with faded Confederate flag stickers on the bumpers of their trucks. The kind of place where two people with blue hair for entirely different reasons might pass on the sidewalk without meeting each other's eyes.

This is a place for ghost stories.

Fredericksburg's home to Civil War battlegrounds and field hospitals. An ancient cemetery lies smack-dab in the middle of the city, commemorating three hundred years of death by disease, cannonball, and bayonet. Women dead in childbirth, farmers stomped to death by horses, slaves shot for no reason at all. Rabies, rotgut booze, the noose. Every square inch of the city's seen its fair share of death, but natural or otherwise, and a good share of those "natural" deaths were probably far less pleasant than the natural ones.

Stands to reason some of them might linger, restless.

Ghost tours were a year-round cottage industry. Wilcox's itself boasted a dozen or more ghost stories I knew of—though none of them were mine. People heard footsteps tramping around the unused third floor of the building or voices whispering in the storage closet. An unseen hand tousled the prep cook's hair in the main basement when he went down to do a line of crystal one morning. One waiter went down to the ancillary basement to get Christmas decorations and quit the very same day without telling anyone—just left a cardboard box of wreaths and tinsel by the back door, didn't even clock out.

I had no such experiences at the restaurant—just the occasional shiver-inducing cold spot I ascribed to the age of the building and the poverty of the HVAC system. Although I *had* seen a few unexplained things in my freshman dorm—near the site of one of those Civil War battles—and the house we'd rented for a year on Wolfe Street lent itself to more than one spooky campfire story, so I wasn't a hardened skeptic when it came to such matters, either.

When Anya and I met, I'd been at Wilcox's for almost three years. Neither of us would work there much longer. I was a year away from fleeing the only state I'd ever known for California; she was probably three or four months from a one-way bus ticket to

New York. Anya wanted to be an actress. Part Italian, part Venezuelan, blessed with a beautiful singing voice and long lashes and a heavily-freckled nose, twentysomething me figured she had a damn good chance of making it. Of course, I was taken with her.

I pretty much had a girlfriend, but she lived an hour away and, with my move imminent, we were prone to breaking up. At the time I was stretching myself across the state, spending Fridays and Saturdays in Richmond with her, Sundays at Wilcox's, and the rest of the week as a file clerk in Old Town Alexandria (between there and Fredericksburg I've had my fucking fill of cobblestone streets). The arrangement led to a lot of driving but allowed me to maintain relationships with friends from undergrad who'd fanned out across the mid-Atlantic after commencement, and let me feel like college wasn't quite over yet.

Anya had a personality way too big for her 5'2" frame. Bursting with energy, competent and knowing, she never got flustered on the floor even when half the town flooded in the doors at once. She floated around the place, toes dangling just above the hollandaise stains on the carpet, singing softly to herself. Mostly top-40 stuff I knew but didn't love—Black Eyed Peas, Justin Timberlake, anything from Casey Kasem's Sunday morning countdown, our constant background noise as we draped the tables in white and arranged the silverware. I didn't have half the voice she did, but a great memory for lyrics, and sometimes when she'd pass by with a tray of poached eggs I'd harmonize.

Things just happened. A simple look. Brushing up against each other at the bread oven. Sharing a joke about a particularly demanding table, or our particularly demanding owner. One night I noticed the dishwasher—a part-time DJ named Grizz—was wearing baggy shorts. The kind that hung down to mid-ankle, nearly kissing the tops of his off-white socks, with big yawning pockets in the back. On a whim, I grabbed a handful of chopped vegetables from the salad station and casually tossed them into his pocket when I walked by the dish pit. I tried the trick a couple more times, and Grizz still didn't notice, arms-deep as he was in soap and scalding water. So I decided to show Anya.

A quick whisper and she was right there on the other side of the big fridge where Annette kept her key lime pies, leaning around the brushed-steel door, watching me slip mushrooms into the dishwasher's JNCOs and trying not to crack up. That kicked off an escalating series of dares, culminating in Anya slipping a freshly-buttered roll into his pocket. As far as I know, Grizz worked the entire shift—and maybe a fucking DJ set after—with a pocketful of chopped veggies and wasn't the wiser until he climbed into his Tercel at the end of the night and finally sat down.

After we got cut, Anya and I had a couple drinks and went back to her place.

Anya's house was across the river in a modern suburban development, centuries removed from the cobblestone streets of downtown Fredericksburg. She lived with her parents, not unusual—I spent part of the week with my parents.

What *was* odd was that her parents were still up.

Two in the morning, we walked in and her mother and father were sitting in the living room, talking to her brother and his girlfriend. Nobody was on drugs, as far as I could tell—they were just night owls. I cringed, shaking hands with everyone. *Meeting the parents* was an event so fraught with significance in my mind I nearly panicked. I'd dated my semi-girlfriend for about a year before she'd met my parents, or I hers. And here I was, on what I thought was a one-night stand, being introduced to everyone of significance in Anya's life like I'd come over for Thanksgiving dinner. Thankfully, we didn't stay long. A few brief and awkward introductions and we went down to her room in the basement.

Sometime later footsteps pattered down the stairs, a door banged open, and then the sounds of her brother and his girlfriend joined with our own through the wall.

In the morning we took our time saying goodbye and then I drove down to Richmond to see my semi-girlfriend and hoped like hell she wouldn't notice the scratches on my back.

Once a week, we were together.

Not the kind of romance epic poems are written about, but for a time it worked. We got along well. Switched shifts so we could work together, and had some fun when the shifts were over.

We shared ambitions—writing, acting, singing. We both wanted to move, not to the same places, but that was okay. She asked me once if I had a girlfriend—I said no.

GHOSTS OF FREDERICKSBURG

Which was technically true, the Richmond girl and I were on a break that wouldn't last.

Meanwhile, Anya had gotten this acting gig, working a few hours a week just down the street from the restaurant, playing a Revolutionary War-era healer at the apothecary shop.

Dating back to the 1700s, the shop was built by a guy named Hugh Mercer—friend of George Washington, physician to his mother, brigadier general in the Continental Army. Now a museum, it sat across the street from a used record store, a storefront church, and a clothier that sold pastel suits and wigs. Anya would tie a bonnet over her curls and put on her petticoat and ruffled gown to regale tourists with stories of bleedings and leechings and all the assorted horrors that constituted colonial medical treatment. I never got to see her in her element, but if she was as good an actor as a singer then I'm sure she was a hit with the school field trips.

One night she told me she was moving to New York. Like she'd planned, like she'd always said, except now she'd set a date—in the next two weeks. We went out drinking, pointedly not talking about the future even though the question loomed between us all night like a balloon at a Catholic school dance. Leave room for Jesus, leave room for doubt. Neither of us wanted to talk about it, we both just wanted to enjoy each other's company, and the fact that we could come to such an easy and unspoken understanding makes me wonder what else could have been.

When the bars closed, I thought we'd go back to her place, but as we wobbled on the sidewalk and took in the deathly quiet town around us, Anya looked at me mischievously and asked if I wanted to go to the apothecary.

Of course I said yes.

We got the key from her car, parked on a side street that gently sloped down to the river. Then she led the way, across streets made of asphalt and cobblestone, past shuttered stores selling assorted bric-a-brac, the sixty-year-old soda fountain Goolrick's, the cozy-yet-perpetually crowded Hyperion coffee shop. In all my years in town, I never did go there.

The apothecary was dark and silent, a small building built in the colonial style but with incongruent aluminum siding that called to mind a horse-drawn buggy with spinning rims, or maybe a laser-sighted blunderbuss. The sign outside said "Shrine Open Daily."

Anya let us in through the back. We walked through a small kitchen area, the break room, and she pulled a flashlight from a drawer. No lights, she told me—the police were prowling the streets at this hour, on the hunt for drunks and vandals.

Besides, it was way more fun with the lights off.

Anya took me down to the basement first, rickety steps swaying under our weight. Unlike the aluminum-sided exterior, the basement walls were formed of rough stone and looked like they'd been built by men in tricorn hats (or more likely hatless men directed by others wearing tricorns). There wasn't much of interest in the basement, so we went back upstairs, into the main room. Boards creaked under our feet, Anya's flashlight revealing a long counter covered in cork-stoppered glass jars, floor to ceiling bookshelves behind, stocked with more jars of all shapes and sizes. Jars, jars, and more jars.

GHOSTS OF FREDERICKSBURG

Anya began to pick up various items of interest, different sorts of colonial remedies and tonics, explaining each as she went. Live leeches. Powdered crab claws. Grisly tools used to amputate gangrenous limbs. She'd shine the light on whatever she was holding, giving me a good long look, and then place it under her chin as she explained what uses the item had, lapsing into the approximated period-speak the docents used. Drunk as I was, I heard half of what she said and retained far less, becoming increasingly disturbed at the sallow complexion the flashlight lent her skin, the speech that was not quite hers. *I don't know who this is,* I remember thinking to myself, my heart hammering its way through all the depressants in my bloodstream.

After a litany of quicksilver and nettle juice and bone saws, we finally went upstairs. The top floor of the apothecary was where the truly sick had lain abed and died. We stood in a short hallway, rooms off to either side blocked by velvet ropes. I craned my head into one—period furniture, twin bed made up with dated linens but turned down like the Ritz, a single window spilling moonlight on the floorboards. I felt Anya at my side, and she asked if I wanted to go lay down in the bed.

Not a bed where anyone had died, surely—those sickly pallets had rotted away centuries before, replaced by the Historical Society with the cheapest options Mattress Discounters had to offer.

Surely.

For a moment I pictured girls in bonnets with baby-swollen bellies, foreheads slick with sweat and faces creased with agony. Old men, moaning through toothless mouths, leeches dotting their necks, sucking what little life they had through papery skin. Poxy children, maimed soldiers, elderly women with bodies like mummies, shriveled, shrinking into their bedclothes.

Anya squeezed my hand, lightly stroked the webbing between my thumb and forefinger.

Of course I said yes.

I lifted a leg over the cordon, but just as my foot crossed the plane—

BAM. BAM. BAM.

From downstairs, or above us, or maybe in the walls. Three times, like someone knocking. Angrily.

I looked at Anya, foot frozen in the air. *What was that?*

She shrugged, said something about water in the pipes.

That must be it, I told myself, not wanting to let my own fears get in the way of the sex story to end all sex stories, the sort of moment I could trot out at the bar from now till doomsday and one-up any of my friends. *Guess what I did, now buy me a shot, loser.*

I let my foot descend another couple inches.

BAM, BAM, BAM. BAM, BAM-BAM.

Heart in my throat, I pulled my foot back and the noise stopped. I looked at Anya, pale in the moonlight.

I think we aren't wanted here.

And then the moonlight shone down on the bed—previously made, I'm sure—but the covers were bunched up down by the bedframe, the sheets covered in dark splotches that called to mind blood, or ichor, and a foul sweet stench, warm and thick, issued forth from the room, choking us, the booze in our stomachs threatening to paint the aged walls.

BAM BAM BAM BAM BAM BAM BAM BAM BAM!

We ran like hell down the stairs, hoping we wouldn't run into whatever was making that noise. No words passed between us. In the kitchen, she slipped the flashlight back in the drawer, the wrong one I think, and we rushed outside, slamming the door behind us.

It took her three or four tries to get the key in the lock.

We drove to her place, stepping right back into the night we thought we'd have, and maybe we kind of talked about it after but I can't remember.

Anya emailed me a couple days after she moved to New York.

A long email, full of details about the city and where she was living and the auditions she hoped to line up, comments on some of the internet articles I'd written. She signed off with an invitation to come see her that weekend and a schedule for the Fung Wah bus, times and locations and costs already researched. All I had to do was buy a ticket.

I didn't.

The weekend she wanted was already taken, by someone else. I wrote her back, told her I couldn't for now, maybe in a few weeks.

We emailed a couple more times, just banalities, but that didn't last long. I was looking west. Pretty soon we stopped talking altogether, and this being the days before social media, that was that.

The other girl and I got back together, acted like

boyfriend and girlfriend despite the expiration date on our relationship. I remember being at some bar in Richmond in the spring, sipping mojitos on the outdoor deck overlooking a pond filled with lily pads. She and her friends in sundresses and floppy hats, watching the night creep in and listening to a guy playing acoustic versions of '90s songs over in the corner. Nurses, all of them. At some point, one of her friends started talking about ghosts. Everybody had some experience or other to share, and I almost chimed in, before I realized I couldn't.

I almost said *yeah, I've got a ghost story.*

But it's not *just* a ghost story. And I couldn't get to the ghosts without wading through a bunch of other stuff that nobody needed to know.

So what I really said was, *I don't believe in any of that stuff. I'm a skeptic.*

And in some ways I am.

Just ask Anya.

AFTERWORD

The collection you've just read includes stories written throughout all stages of my career. Some are previously published, like "Seven Years Bad Luck" in *If I Die Before I Wake: Tales of Nightmare Creatures* and "Stool Pigeon" in *Kelp*. Some are stories I wrote years ago, like "Preservation," which never quite found a home (although this version is quite a bit different than the original), while "Faces of Death" was written exclusively for this collection. All are stories I'm quite proud of, and happy to be sharing them with you.

Which brings us to "The Siren Song of Sharp and Deadly Things."

Back in 2018, my friend and hype man Max Booth III announced he was doing a pizza horror anthology. How the hell do you write a pizza horror story? Max challenged the indie horror community to figure that one out, and if the sheer number of "no pizza stories" in magazine submission guidelines is any indication, he literally changed the industry forever.

Slow clap.

Now, one thing you should know about me, which is not the most interesting factoid in the world because it applies to pretty much goddamn everybody: I love pizza. Ever since I was a baby ninja turtle, I've been obsessed with it. One of my favorite places on the planet is the 4th Horseman in Long Beach, CA, a horror-themed pizza joint that's got some of the best pies I've ever had (plus a great tap list). I love this place so much that during the earliest days of the pandemic, my girlfriend at the time and I drove three hours round trip just to grab takeout.

But I digress (see, this is what happens when people mention pizza). When I saw Max's submission call, I knew I wanted in. But like I said, how the hell do you write a pizza horror story? Around the same time, I was doomscrolling Facebook and came across a post from writer Richard Thomas about the French concept of l'Appel du Vide, or the Call of the Void. If you've ever been standing on an apartment balcony or walking along a cliff or even forced to park on the highest level of a parking garage, you might have felt it—that feeling when you realize you *could* jump, a flimsy-looking railing the only thing separating you from a multi-story fall and accompanying *splat*. It's terrifying, especially because it's bizarrely not a form of suicidal ideation, it has more to do with wires in your brain getting crossed—seriously, google it, it's super fascinating.

I've felt that feeling, standing on the fourteenth-floor balcony of a high-rise overlooking Lindbergh Field, or a hiking trail out in Jamacha. At the damn mall, even, looking down on the food court from the second floor. Scared the hell out of me. They say write what scares you, so I did. What if someone heard the Call of the Void everywhere they went? What would their life be like?

That kernel of an idea became "The Siren Song of Sharp and Deadly Things."

The story didn't make the cut for the pizza anthology—which you should totally check out, by the way, it's called *Tales From the Crust*—and every magazine (rightfully) closed their doors to leftover pizza horror. But I still loved the story, so I held onto it, hoping one day I'd find the right way to share it with readers.

And I did. Whether you loved it, hated it, or skipped right over, I'm incredibly stoked that this piece—one of the most unique and personal I've written, I think—is out there in the world.

And I'm very glad to share it with you.

ACKNOWLEDGMENTS

"I know in a way I never knew before that there is nowhere for me to go, nothing for me to do, and no one for me to know."
—Thomas Ligotti, "The Bungalow House"

There's a bunch of people I usually thank on this page, and those are always people I'm grateful for, but when it comes down to it, for this particular collection of stories, there's one person I owe a special thank you—the same writer to whom I dedicated this book, Thomas Ligotti.

You've seen the inscription in the opening pages, but I'd be remiss if I didn't expound a bit on what that means. It's a paraphrase from Ligotti's story "The Bungalow House," perhaps one of his bleakest, and that's saying something.

It's also one of the reasons I bother writing in the first place.

The story's about a guy who works at the library and spends his lunch breaks in an art gallery. Becomes obsessed with these odd tape recordings of an artist doing monologues about crumbling, vermin-infested places. I'm not going to spoil the ending, but the story expertly dissects our relationship with art and the paradoxes inherent when we experience it, and is so wonderfully constructed you could spend days unpacking it. When I think about what Ligotti's work "means," it's definitely one of the foremost examples, one of the most "pure" (although I'd rank "Purity" and "Vastarien" up there as some of his absolute best arguments). The quote about nothing to do, nowhere to go, and no one to know is one of the most succinct summations of what anhedonia actually is—a condition I've grappled with on and off throughout my life, and essentially amounts to an inability to take pleasure in life. When I was formally diagnosed in 2008, that just led to more questions. Mine's of a mild variety, and I do get long periods of relief, but when I'm in it—and when I am, it feels endless—I need something to hold on to. Why persevere, if you're just going through the motions? If you take no pleasure in what you're doing, no matter what it is?

Ligotti's work—and more importantly his continued production of it over several decades—answers those questions in such incredibly satisfying ways. That feeling of there being nowhere to go, nothing to do, and no one to know? At root is the inabilty to appreciate distinctions. The feeling that everywhere, everything, and everyone is fundamentally the same on the most base level, which is perhaps the best example of something that is at once unassailably true and incontroveribly false I've ever heard. It's like in *We Need to Talk About Kevin,* when Lionel Shriver's Eva declares all places exist on the "shoes/weather continuum," meaning all places and cultures have customs regarding shoes, and all experience weather, and so why should one care? Yes, some customs or weather are extreme (like spending hundreds of dollars on sneakers or enduring hurricane season), but because all places have those things, there's a sense of sameness.

No matter where you go.

No matter what you do there, or who you talk to.

When you recognize that, how can you derive enjoyment from a trip or an activity or a conversation, knowing everything is just a matter of degree?

Maybe you can't. But people like Thomas Ligotti—and to a much lesser degree, myself—persist, and when I feel like there's no enjoyment to be had from life?

I keep going anyway.

ABOUT THIS DUDE

Brian Asman is a writer, editor, producer, and actor from San Diego, CA. He's the author of *I'm Not Even Supposed to Be Here Today* from Eraserhead Press, and *Man, Fuck This House, Nunchuck City,* and *Jailbroke* from Mutated Media. He's recently published short stories in the anthologies *Breaking Bizarro, Welcome to the Splatter Club,* and *Lost Films,* and comics in *Tales of Horrorgasm.* He co-wrote the film *A Haunting in Ravenwood,* now available on DVD and VOD. He holds an MFA from the University of California, Riverside at Palm Desert. He's represented by Dunham Literary, Inc. Max Booth III is his hype man.

IF YOU DUG THIS . . .

CHECK OUT
MAN, FUCK THIS HOUSE,
AVAILABLE NOW FROM MUTATED MEDIA

With his "highly visual and cinematic worldbuilding" (Booklife by Publishers Weekly), Brian Asman spins a horrifying and imaginative tale of an ordinary family and their extraordinary new house . . .

Sabrina Haskins and her family have just moved into their dream home, a gorgeous Craftsman in the rapidly-growing Southwestern city of Jackson Hill. Sabrina's a bored and disillusioned homemaker, Hal a reverse mortgage salesman with a penchant for ill-timed sports analogies. Their two children, Damien and Michaela, are bright and precocious.

At first glance, the house is perfect. But things aren't what they seem.

Sabrina's hearing odd noises, seeing strange visions. Their neighbors are odd or absent. And Sabrina's already-fraught relationship with her son is about to be tested in a way no parent could ever imagine.

Because while the Haskins family might be the newest owners of 4596 James Circle, they're far from its only residents . . .

Made in the USA
Las Vegas, NV
12 April 2022